No Good Deed

Kathy Hamilton Mystery Series

Killer Deception

Hush Now, Don't Cry

No Good Deed

Maggie Casteen

No Good Deed

ISBN 978-1-66784-550-0

Cover stock photos used with permission
smoke image by cottonbro from pexels,
bloody handprint by gerait from pixabay,
and crime scene tape by Kat Wilcox from pexels.
Back cover crime scene tape photo by Kat Wilcox.
Cover design by Maggie Casteen, author.

Bookbaby Publishing
7905 N. Crescent Blvd.
Pennsauken, NJ 08110
www.bookbaby.com

Frist Edition
Printed in the United States of America

"While all deception requires secrecy,
all secrecy is not meant to deceive."

~Sissela Bok

Prologue

Thursday, April 17th

The sun was slowly going down as Charlie walked into his hideout at the abandoned mall. He had lived there for four years now, the longest he had stayed in one place. He looked around and saw that Rose and Simon weren't there. They were probably trying to find something to eat before it got too late. Charlie leaned against one of the concrete columns as he waited. He had called Kathy to try and meet him one more time, but it went straight to voicemail.

"This time, I'm not running," he reassured himself, "I'm done...it's just not right. I have to tell the..." he suddenly felt something sharp pointing into his back.

"You know," the voice said softly "what they don't know, won't hurt them." Charlie's eyes grew wide as he realized what was happening. Before Charlie could say a word, he felt his world go dark.

When he woke up his head was splitting, and his

hands were tied. Charlie slowly raised his head to find a man squatting in front of him. The shadows of the building hid most of him except for his eyes. The blackness in his eyes made Charlie start to sweat, now he knew how that girl felt.

"You've been a problem for me," the man said matter-of-factly. "I don't like problems. So, here's what's going to happen. I am going to ask you a question, and if you don't give me the truth, well...," a smile crept onto his face, "it's gonna get very interesting for you. However, if you do, I'll make it as painless as possible." Charlie suddenly forgot how to breathe. "Now, who were you calling?" he asked as he pulled a knife from his coat pocket. Charlie tried to swallow but his throat was so dry.

"I..." Charlie stammered, "I was...calling someone, but she didn't pick up."

The man smiled, "Name."

"I'm not sure of her name." Charlie stammered as the man moved closer.

"Hmm, let's see if I can help you with that," he said as he pointed the knife to the side of his face and slowly pressed down.

"Kathy," Charlie blurted out, "I was calling Kathy Hamilton, but she didn't pick up."

"Thank you," the man said as Charlie's eyes began to tear up. This was not how he wanted to go; there were so many things he still wanted to do, things that needed to be resolved. Charlie's life replayed in his head like a movie, the moments he would treasure and the face of the person he loved most. *I love you, Alyssa*, he thought to himself as he desperately wished for someone to save him. "Now that we have concluded our business, how would you like to die?" Charlie bowed his head as a tear slowly ran down his face. The man slowly bent toward him as he whispered in his ear, "Hush now, don't cry."

Friday, April 18th

1

Kathy woke up as the sound of her alarm clock rang in her ear. She wiped the sleep from her eyes and hit the 'off' button for the alarm. She looked around and still couldn't believe that she had actually moved into the apartment. She looked at the clock on her phone which read seven-thirty and noticed that she had a voicemail message. Kathy hit the button and typed in her four-digit password. Kathy's eyes went wide as the message began to play.

> *Miss Kathy, it's Charlie. I know I didn't show up, but I need to talk to you. Meet me at the same place at nine. I need to tell the truth.*

Kathy noticed the date and time of the message. Charlie had called while they were at Christine's.

"Crap," she said as she threw off the covers "maybe, he's still there," she said as she threw on a pair of jeans and a T-shirt. She carefully put her locket on and grabbed her bag that was lying on the desk chair. Kathy quickly left a note for Stacey on the fridge as she hurried out the door. *Please, Charlie*, she thought to herself, *don't leave me hanging again.*

2

As Kathy pulled into the parking lot of the abandoned mall, she took a quick glance around. She didn't see anybody, but maybe he was waiting inside. Kathy slowly got out and cautiously made her way to the back door of the building. She felt goosebumps creep on her arms, but she quickly brushed it off. As she stepped inside, she looked around.

"Charlie," she called out, "it's Kathy. I know I'm really late, but I'm here now." Kathy slowly walked forward hoping for a reply. "Charlie please talk to...," Kathy stopped dead in her tracks and let out a gasp. Charlie was there, but he wouldn't be talking today. Kathy looked in horror as she saw Charlie slumped over against a concrete column. There was blood all over his shirt, and his arms were lying there lifeless at his sides. She started to go over to him but stopped herself. She dug out her cell and made a quick call.

"This is Bailey Clark," the voice said.

"Bailey," Kathy said weakly.

"Kathy, what's wrong?"

"I was meeting Charlie, I mean I was supposed to meet him last night, but I didn't get the message and..."

"What?" Bailey asked getting worried.

"Bailey...he's dead," Kathy finally said.

"Kathy, listen to me," he said sternly "don't touch anything. Call the police, give them a statement, and then come here and we'll figure it out."

"Okay," Kathy said taking a deep breath.

"You, okay?"

"Yeah, I got it," she said as she hung up. Kathy looked at Charlie and kicked herself. She quickly took two pictures and then called 911 as the operator answered.

"911, what is your emergency?"

Kathy took a breath, "My name is Kathy Hamilton, and I'd like to report a murder. I'm at the abandoned mall right outside of town."

"Okay, ma'am. Stay on the line with me. I'm sending help right now." *Help,* Kathy thought to herself; there would be no help for Charlie. It was too late for him.

3

Kathy waited in her car as she saw a police car pull up. She got out and saw that the officers were Michael and Jamie. *Well, at least I've got a friendly face to talk to*, she thought as they came over.

"Hey guys," she said as Jamie pulled out a notepad.

"Are you okay?" Michael said trying to stay professional.

"Yeah, I'm alright."

"You talk to Jamie, and I'll go and secure the scene," Michael said as he took a roll of police tape and walked away.

"So, what happened?" Jamie began.

"I had gotten a voicemail from Charlie. I was supposed to meet him here yesterday at nine, but I didn't get the message till this morning. So, I came straight over, walked to the back door, and looked around. That's when I saw him."

"What time did you get here?"

"A little after nine, maybe."

"Did you see anybody else?"

"No."

"Why did he want to meet?"

"Charlie was, I think, a witness to the murder of Sandra Malone, and he was calling because he said he wanted to tell the truth."

"He didn't say anything else?"

Kathy shook her head, "No, just to meet him." Jamie saw that Kathy was starting to get emotional.

"Okay, I think that's enough for now. I'd ask for contact information, but I'm pretty sure my partner already has that." Kathy gave a small smile as they saw Michael walking toward them.

"All done?" he asked as Jamie put away his notepad.

"I think so," Jamie said.

"Hey, Kathy," Michael began, "did you notice anything about Charlie?"

Kathy looked puzzled, "No, what do you mean?"

Michael took a step closer, "There was something written in the dirt beside the body."

"What?" Kathy replied shocked.

"It said, I saw him," Michael replied.

"Holy crap. I didn't see anything like that. I guess the dead body and bloody clothes kinda drew my attention," Kathy said defensively.

"No big deal," Michael reassured her. "I was just asking if it was there when you walked in."

"I'm sorry, Michael. I'm just..." Kathy shook her head. Michael took her hand, "It's okay. Nobody sees everything," he said with a reassuring smile. Kathy nodded and smiled in return. "Where are you headed now?" he asked concerned.

"Bailey's" Kathy replied, "I think I need to talk to someone who can make some sense of this."

"Sounds good," Michael said as he walked her to her car. "Hey," he said as she looked up, "call me if you need me."

"I love you too," Kathy said as she got in her car and started the ignition. Kathy desperately hoped that Bailey's calm manner would help her make sense of what had happened.

4

Kathy walked into the office building and went straight to Bailey's office. Her mind was spinning; she felt like she was walking in a dream, and hopefully soon, she would wake up and realize none of this had happened. She knocked on Bailey's door and walked in when she heard his voice.

Bailey was behind his desk and asked her to have a seat. Kathy plopped down in one of the leather chairs across from him. She still had no idea what to say.

"Okay" Bailey stated, "now what exactly happened from the very beginning?"

Kathy nodded, "It started this morning; I woke up and saw that I had a message last night. So, I listen to it, and it was Charlie."

"What time was that message?" he asked jotting down

some notes.

"He left it while we were at Christine's celebrating. I guess that's why I didn't hear it. Anyway, he said he wanted to meet at the same place."

"Where was that?" Bailey interjected.

"The abandoned mall; he stays there sometimes. So, I go right over there, and I go in the back like I did last time. There's nobody there that I saw, so I call out and keep looking until... there he was."

"Anything else?"

"No. I called you, then waited for the police to show up," she said with a puzzled look on her face.

"What is it?"

"The police unit turned out to be Michael and Jamie, and Michael said that Charlie had written something before he died."

Bailey stopped writing, "Really?"

"He wrote I saw him in the dirt. What do you think it means?" Bailey leaned back in his chair and thought for a moment.

"It could be he was trying to leave you a message."

"Charlie wanted to tell me what he saw that night. Maybe that was his way of letting me know."

"It's hard to say, but to me, this is more evidence that Chase didn't kill Sandra Malone." Kathy nodded in agreement.

"The question now is who did Charlie see?"

"I don't have a clue," Kathy replied frustrated. "So now, what happens?"

Bailey looked at his watch, "Now we order some lunch and discuss what you will say in court." The color drained from Kathy's face.

"Bailey, please tell me you're joking."

"Sorry, but you did find the body. More than likely, you will be at the top of the list to testify." Bailey said as he dialed Sally at the front desk. Bailey put in their lunch order as Kathy stared at the floor. She cringed at the thought of being in a courtroom. "Kathy?" Bailey said getting her to look up, "don't worry. I doubt you're a suspect, you'll just have to answer some basic questions that's all."

"I sure hope you're right," she said hopefully.

As they went over word by word what Kathy needed to say, Sally brought the lunches in and placed them on Bailey's desk.

"Oh, Kathy, before I forget, this came for you," Sally said and handed Kathy an envelope with Kathy's name on the front.

"Thanks," she said putting it in her pocket, "I'll look at it later. Right now, I'm starved." Sally smiled as she walked out to return to her post at the front desk. Kathy took the burger and fries that Bailey handed her and immediately took the pickles off her burger.

"No pickles, huh?" Bailey said with a smile.

"No, I just can't," she replied as she took a bite.

"Alright," Bailey said wiping his hands with a napkin, "we've gone over what happened and what led up to you finding the body. I think we've done a decent job on what the prosecution may ask you."

"I just cringe at the thought of being questioned by D.A. Phillips."

"I don't blame you for that, but don't get too upset. Remember you are not a suspect, just a witness."

Kathy nodded, "Got it. I think I'll take the rest of this to my desk," she said gathering what was left of her lunch, "I think I just need a moment to myself."

Bailey smiled, "I understand," he said as Kathy went to her office across the hallway and sat down behind her desk.

She put her lunch in front of her as the events of the day replayed over and over in her head. As she searched for her desk keys, she found the letter Sally had given her.

"Let's see what this is," she said as she opened it up. Kathy pulled out a white sheet of paper with a simple message written on it.

No good deed goes unpunished.

-W

Kathy re-read the message again. "What?" she asked softly not sure what to make of it. Kathy sat there with the note lying on her desk staring at her. *What does this mean?* she thought to herself, *what is going on?* Kathy could not begin to contemplate the meaning of those words or the evil intent behind them.

5

Dr. Hamilton sat in the waiting room trying to figure out what to say. He had plenty of thoughts; he just didn't know how to put them into words.

"Commander Winters will see you now," the secretary said as Dr. Hamilton got up and followed her to Commander Winter's office. She opened the door and escorted him in as Commander Winters got up and extended his hand.

"Hello, David. It's nice to see you again," he said as they both took a seat. "How is everything?"

"Pretty good, uh, Kathy just got a job as an investigator." Commander Winters smiled, "Yes, I heard about that. From an unnamed source, of course."

David finally let out a smile, "Nice office you have here. You've really climbed the ranks."

"Yes, well, there's pros and cons to everything. Now, how can I help you?"

David took a breath, "Commander Winter..."

"James, please. My subordinates here call me commander," he interjected.

"James, I know it's been several years since I've brought up my wife's case, but I have to ask. Will it ever be solved?"

James leaned forward in his chair, "I could give you a politically correct answer, but I won't do that. The hard truth is that Colleen's murder has been cold for so many years and with no new leads.....the chances are just not that good." David suspected that would be the answer, but it was still hard to hear.

"Do you think a fresh set of eyes would help?" he asked hopefully.

"It wouldn't hurt. If you've found anything at all let me know," he said handing David his card, "and I will see to it personally." James paused for a moment. "David, it has always bothered me that I couldn't give your family justice. I tried everything. I promise you that if you find anything, no matter how small, I will re-open the Colleen Hamilton case."

David's eyes started to get moist as he tried to blink them away. "Thank you. That means everything to us. I would like to ask one more thing before I go."

"Name it."

"Don't tell Kathy about this. I don't want her to get her hopes up and then be disappointed, again."

James held up his hand, "I understand," he said as he

walked David to the door. "If I can help in any way, let me know."

"Thank you," he said shaking his hand.

"I wish you the best," he said as David turned and walked down the hallway out of sight. James returned to his office and sat down behind his desk. The Colleen Hamilton case was the only case he had never solved. A thorn in his side and a mark on his near-perfect record. He still remembered it; everything was so clear after all these years. He didn't want to give false hope to David and Kathy, but James knew in his heart that the Colleen Hamilton case would never be solved.

6

Kathy had picked up some supper from Masconi's Little Italy on the way back to the apartment. She had put the note back in her bag for the time being. As she opened the door to the apartment, she heard Stacey's pop music fill the air.

"Food is on the table," she called out as she placed the take-out bags on the dining room table.

"Smells great," Stacey said as she turned down the music and headed for the table.

"How do you write with that stuff playing?" she asked as she grabbed two sodas from the fridge.

Stacey grinned, "Don't you know that upbeat music makes you work better?"

"Maybe for you," Kathy replied opening the box containing her cheese ravioli, "so what is the current assignment?"

"Just brainstorming right now," Stacey replied opening her chicken alfredo, "you left early this morning."

"No" Kathy interrupted, "you sleep too late."

Stacey smiled, "Possibly, and no you can't quote me on that." Kathy laughed. "So, what was the hurry this morning?"

"Where do I start?"

"At the very beginning" Stacey interrupted, "and don't leave out anything," she said giving Kathy her full attention.

"I had gotten a message from Charlie to meet him last night."

"Charlie, you mean the Charlie you've been looking for."

"Yeah, the same one. Anyway, I didn't get the message till this morning, so I rush over there, and I don't see anybody."

"Not again!" Stacey huffed.

"Wait, I keep going and I do find him this time."

"That's great!"

"Only he's dead."

Stacey's face dropped, "Well, that's not so great. What happened?" she asked taking a bite.

"It looks like he had been stabbed and there was blood all over his clothes."

"What did you do?"

"I called Bailey. I didn't want to do something stupid."

Stacey grinned, "Smart move."

"I'm so glad you approve."

"Then what?"

"The police came, and it so happened to be Michael and Jamie."

"Well, aren't you the lucky one?" Stacey remarked with a wink.

Kathy rolled her eyes, "The point is that Michael told me that Charlie had written I saw him in the dirt."

"Holy crap!" Stacey replied as she wiped her mouth with a napkin. "So, what does that mean?"

"I think it has to do with the fact that Charlie wanted to tell me who really killed Sandra Malone."

"Well, you certainly had an eventful day."

"Tell me about it, and to top it off, Bailey says I'll have to testify."

"Ooh, I am sorry about that," Stacey said seriously, "no way out, huh?"

"I don't think so," Kathy said as she threw away her trash. "Anyway, I think I'll take a hot shower and just chill out in my room."

"Okay," Stacey replied taking the rest of her food to her desk. "I'll be right here brainstorming a masterpiece."

Kathy shook her head as she headed toward her room. She really needed the hot water to wash away the day, but that note still loomed in the back of her mind. She wasn't quite sure why she didn't tell Stacey about it. *Maybe it'll just go away,* she thought. She hoped that would be the case.

Saturday, April 19th

7

It was a beautiful Saturday morning when Michael picked Kathy up at Riverside Apartments. They had decided to spend the day together and Kathy was very excited. She had tried to call her dad yesterday as well, but it went straight to voicemail. Kathy thought that was strange, but she decided to brush it off. *He probably just didn't hear the phone,* she thought, as she headed downstairs to wait for Michael. With everything going on, Kathy jumped at the chance for a distraction, especially one as good-looking as Michael Winters. She smiled when his black GMC Sierra pulled up; she hopped into the front seat and leaned back determined to enjoy the day.

"So, where to first?" Michael asked pulling out of the parking lot.

"Well, I wanted to go to the bookstore. I have a lot of

empty shelves and I need to fill them," she saw the strained look on Michael's face, "which is why I need an expert opinion on what I should get," she said with a grin.

"As long as it's far away from the fiction section," he said as they turned out of the Riverside parking lot.

They walked into the Bookmark Bookshop minutes later, and Kathy went straight for the non-fiction section with Michael trailing slowly behind. The Bookmark was a small bookshop in the Rosemont mall with a vintage feel to it. The owners, Alice and Paul, had taken over for Alice's parents and had continued running it in the same family tradition. Kathy maneuvered her way through the bookcases to the law and criminology section to begin her browsing. Michael watched Kathy carefully as she browsed the numerous titles. He didn't notice any difference in her behavior, but maybe, it was just too soon to tell. After the situation yesterday, he had called her late last night to see how she was doing. He couldn't detect any signs of shock, but he would keep a close eye on her. If he had any say about it, nothing would hurt her that he had already decided.

"I see you found it," Michael said as he watched in amusement as Kathy closely examined the books.

"Which one do you think is best?" she asked holding up two paperbacks. Michael gave them both an honest look.

"I'd go with *Robeson's Guide to Private Investigators* over the *Idiot's Guide to P.I.*"

"Really?" she said looking at them again. "Yeah, you're probably right," she said putting the other one back on the shelf.

"So, what else would be good to have?" Michael casually browsed the shelves until he found two that he considered being useful and handed them to Kathy.

Kathy noted both titles, "*The Handbook of Detectives* and *Fact-Finding: Things to know for solving any case,*" she smiled. "See, I knew you would be perfect for this," she said as she placed them both in her stack. She kept browsing until she stopped dead in her tracks. "That's it!" she said as Michael came over to see what Kathy had found. Kathy held up a small hardback book. "This is it, the perfect book for a detective," she said handing it to Michael.

"*How To Think Like Holmes*," he read out loud. "You think a book can teach you that?" he asked sarcastically as Kathy took the book back.

"You never know," she said with a wink.

"Alright, Sherlock. So does that make me Watson?" Kathy giggled.

"Well, we'll see...it's a close call between you and Stacey."

"Ah, I'm crushed," he said with a mocked expression, "So, is lunch next on the schedule. I'm starting to get hungry."

"Well, I guess," she said picking up her stack of books off the floor, "and I know the perfect place."

"How do you know that?" he said following her to the check-out counter.

Kathy stopped and turned around, "Why it's elementary, of course," as they both laughed.

8

Dr. Hamilton hadn't slept well; his mind was too preoccupied with Colleen. He had eaten a quick bite for breakfast and then made the trip to the attic the dark place where Colleen's things were kept. It had been a little over ten years since he had been up here. He thought he had heard the phone ring, but he ignored it Colleen was waiting. He pushed some boxes aside until he found what he was looking for; two white boxes marked Colleen's Office. He brushed away the years of dust and tenderly carried them out of the attic.

He sat them down in the hallway as his eyes began to glisten. Even after all these years, the pain was still there, a hole that would never be filled. He opened one of the boxes and started thumbing through the hodge-podge of papers: files, notepads, and old crinkled post-it notes.

Somewhere in here has to be the answer, he thought, *there is an answer, and I will find it.* He took both boxes to his office and slid them under his desk, out of sight. Then he went over to his desktop to do some research.

"Where to start?" he asked softly. He didn't have the first clue about hiring an investigator. "Well, I'll go at it like I do one of my projects," he finally decided. "I've never met a problem that I couldn't solve and this one will be no different. The investigator I need is out there, and I will find him."

9

Kathy had tried to call her dad again, but it ended up in his voicemail again.

"What's wrong?" Michael asked as they were leaving Delany's.

"I was just trying to touch base with Dad, but he didn't pick up," she said with a puzzled look on her face.

"I wouldn't worry about it," he said gathering her in his arms, "he's probably focused on his latest project. I know how tunnel vision works when it comes to the Hamiltons," he said with a grin.

Kathy giggled, "I will take that as a compliment," she said as she kissed him. "I just hope he's okay now that I've moved out."

"He's fine," Michael said reassuringly, "but there is

something I wanted to mention."

"What's that?" Kathy said as they hopped inside Michael's truck.

"Now that you're an investigator, there's going to be more..." he searched for the right word, "unpredictable situations."

Kathy peered up over at him, "And..."

"And I wanted you to, umm... have you ever thought about a self-defense class or some kind of protection?" he said waiting for her reaction.

"A self-defense class?" she repeated, thinking it over.

"Yeah. I mean at least you would have some way to protect..." Kathy leaned over and kissed him.

"You're worried about me, aren't you?"

"I am just trying to be practical," he paused. "I might be a little worried. Just think about it. I mean finding Charlie like that, there could've easily been someone hiding somewhere, and things could've escalated very quickly." Kathy saw the worried look in his eyes and smiled.

"Okay, I'll think about it, but no more shop talk. I want to be distracted today, so, where to next?" she said. Michael gave a sly smile.

"If it's a distraction you're after, I know the perfect place," he replied as he pulled out of Delany's parking lot.

Kathy looked at him skeptically, "Really, please do tell."

Michael grinned, "The Retro Arcade."

"Oh no," she said laughing.

"Oh, yes. There is everything you could ever want there, even funnel cakes and...."

"Don't say it," Kathy said trying not to grin.

"Foosball."

"You know I'm addicted to that game, right?"

"Oh, my bad," he said grinning.

"You're terrible," she said smiling, "Fine, lead the way, and if I crush you again, don't come crying to me."

"See that's what I love most about you. You're just all heart," he said as they both laughed.

10

Winchester was calmly resting in his motel room quietly, celebrating his success. He stared up at the grey ceiling, replaying the scene over. He had stayed for a moment or two watching as Charlie slowly slipped away. *Another problem solved,* he thought to himself, *and no one will ever know that I was there.* The cell phone on the nightstand began to vibrate. Winchester knew who it was; he picked it up still lying on the bed.

"“Yes,” he said calmly.

“Is our problem solved?” the voice asked.

“Yes sir, all wrapped up,” he said with a small grin.

“Good, Winchester, that’s better. Did you make sure somebody else will take the fall?”

“Sure thing, boss. The evidence will lead the police to an easy arrest.”

"Stay there until you know for sure then call me. I might have another situation for you to handle."

"Fine," he said as the voice hung up. Winchester put the cell phone back on the nightstand as he went to the mini-fridge and grabbed a beer. He was always handling some situation, people screwed up, and they sent him to fix it.

He turned on the TV as the news was just coming on. It was another report about the Charles Goldson murder. Winchester started to change the channel when a shot of Kathy Hamilton came on the screen. Winchester analyzed her face and couldn't decide what it was about her that was familiar. S*he was a pretty little thing*, Winchester thought, as he finished his beer. *What is it about that Kathy girl?* he wondered, as he laid back down to take a nap.

11

After three hours of indoor basketball, Street Fighter, and of course, foosball, Kathy and Michael decided they had had enough. As usual, Kathy had won the foosball competition, and so, he spilt the difference with the indoor basketball.

"That was great!" Kathy said as they walked out of the arcade their arms around each other.

"Told you....a classic never fails," he said with a smile.

"I guess I should be getting back."

"Don't say that," he said pulling her closer, "I had something else planned."

Kathy peered up at him, "Really, what's that?"

"Movie at my place," he said with a kiss. Kathy thought about it and saw those warm brown eyes looking back at her. *How does he do it,* she thought to herself. Kathy shook her head in defeat.

"Well, I guess it's not the worst idea if..."

"If what?"

"If there's cheese pizza in the deal."

"Dialing the number as you speak," he said pulling out his phone as Kathy laughed.

* * * * * * * *

Kathy and Michael walked into his studio apartment at Meadow Gardens. As she placed the hot pizza box on the living room coffee table, she looked around and grinned. Hardly anything on the walls, which were a standard grey color.
"You know you could do with a picture or two," she commented as Michael closed the door.

"I'll make a note of it," he said as he pulled the movie from his collection. Kathy took a seat on the dark grey sofa as Michael put the movie in.

"Do I dare ask?"

Michael took a seat beside her, "Something for both of us, an action mystery movie, *Outside the Law*," he said grabbing a piece of pizza. Kathy smiled as she snuggled in as the movie started. She laid her head on his shoulder and forgot all about the pizza. She sighed and knew she wanted to stay like this forever.

Sunday, April 30th

12

Kathy didn't get back to the apartment until ten o'clock the next morning. She quietly opened the door and slowly closed it behind her. As she started to tip-toe down the hallway, she heard Stacey's music and knew she was sunk. Stacey was at her desk typing away as Kathy came into view. Stacey looked up and smiled.

"Well, hello stranger," she said as she stopped typing and turned to face her roommate. Kathy threw her bag on the sofa and kicked off her shoes.

"Hey, Stace."

"Now, I'm not a detective," she said with a sly smile, "but I believe yesterday you spent all day with Michael and you're just coming in now so...." her voice trailed off. Kathy just stood there trying not to smile.

"So?"

"So, tell me everything," Stacey said exasperated. Kathy laughed and pulled up a chair beside her desk.

"Well, Michael and I did spend the whole day together, so congratulations on your deft deduction. Then, I had mentioned that I probably should be getting back and that's when he mentioned the movie."

"And?"

"And so, we went back to his place with the pizza we had picked up. I sat on the couch, and he sat down beside me. Then as the movie started, I snuggled up on his shoulder."

"Uh-huh," Stacey said with bated breath.

"He slowly put his arm around me and ..."

"Oh, come on, don't leave me hanging."

"And then the next thing I knew, I fell asleep." Stacey's face fell as she looked dumbstruck at her roommate.

"Excuse me, I think I misheard you. Can you repeat that last part again?"

Kathy just shrugged her shoulders, "I fell asleep." Stacey threw up her hands in disgust.

"Ah, Kathy, say it ain't so. Please tell me, how do you fall asleep with a six-foot, drop-dead gorgeous officer sitting next to you?" she said in disbelief.

"I guess I was just tired from all the stuff we did yesterday. It felt really nice and when I woke up, he had put a pillow under my head and a blanket over me. Wasn't that sweet?" Stacey just shook her head.

"If it was me, that boy would not be sleeping," she said with a grin.

"Well, you won't have to worry about it because he's all mine."

"Yes, we know."

"So, what have you been up to?" Kathy asked changing the subject. Stacey scooted back in front of her computer and pulled up her latest assignment.

"While I was hoping to get the Charlie murder story since I have such a good source," she said peeking up at Kathy, "that was given to somebody else, and I am stuck with the candidate profiles for the upcoming town council election."

"That could still be interesting."

"We'll see. They are politicians, and there's got to be at least one of them with an interesting story."

"I'm sure you have it under control," Kathy said with a wink.

"Hopefully, I won't have to do many more pieces like this before I start getting the good assignments," Stacey said as she looked at the cube clock on her desk. "It's about break time. So, what's for lunch?"

"Just order our usual Chinese," Kathy said walking away, "I've got to see if I can get a hold of Dad first."

"Homesick already?" she said jokingly.

"No, I've just tried to call him twice yesterday, and they both went to voicemail."

"Mmmm, I'll take care of the food and you can handle

that," Stacey replied as Kathy walked into her room. *It was strange that he didn't pick up,* Kathy thought as she dialed his number again, hoping everything was okay.

13

Dr. Hamilton had spent all morning online researching private investigators. The different kinds of investigators varied about as much as the cost to hire one. As he continued to scroll through the list, one finally caught his eye. It read *'Private Eye for Hire. Twenty years of experience will travel,* and the part that he focused on was, *won't stop till we have an answer.'* He clicked on the link and a contact page pulled up for Todd Rainor, a private investigator located in New York. As he jotted down the number the phone rang.

"Hello?" he said distracted.

"Hi, Dad." Dr. Hamilton dropped the pen he was holding.

"Hi sweetie, how are you?"

"I was getting ready to ask you the same thing. I tried

calling you twice yesterday. You're not working on Saturdays now, are you?" she teased. Dr. Hamilton silently kicked himself, he had heard the phone ring, but he was too caught up going through Colleen's things.

"Sorry about that. I was in my home office, and I just didn't hear it." He hated the fact that he was keeping Kathy in the dark, but it was for the best.

"Oh, okay. I just wanted to check-in and make sure everything was good."

"Uh-huh, I'm fine. Don't worry about me. Although, if you wanted to stop by for dinner one night..." he hinted.

Kathy giggled, "I'll see what I can do about that. Okay, well talk to you soon," she said as she hung up.

"Bye sweetie," he said and put the phone down. The contact information for Todd Rainor was staring at him on the screen. He sat down and took out his cell phone and dialed the number. *What do I say,* he thought, *will he even take the case? At least money is not a problem. I'll pay whatever it costs if I can just get the answer I need.* He slowly took a deep breath as the phone started to ring.

"Todd Rainor, private investigator," a man's voice answered.

"Hello. My name is David Hamilton and I was... My wife was murdered several years ago, and I need help in getting some answers."

"Can you give me a little more information? Where did this happen?"

"In North Carolina, a town called Rosemont. It's where I

still live."

"And you say the case is now cold?"

"Yes. The police can't do anything. Will you take the case?"

"I've just finished up with my last client, so here's the deal. My fee upfront is $1,000 and after that, it's $100 a day. I'll email you an agreement of services and if it is acceptable, just sign and send it back. We'll work out the details when I get there."

"You said $1,000 upfront."

"Is that a problem?"

"No, money is not a problem. I just wanted to make sure I had the amount right." Dr. Hamilton gave Todd his email address and Todd said he would send the agreement within the hour. He also told Dr. Hamilton that he would be on the next flight out once the agreement was returned. They both agreed, and Dr. Hamilton hung up the phone. He couldn't believe that he had actually done it, after years of nothing, something was finally moving forward. He was moving one step closer to finally knowing what happened to his beautiful Colleen.

14

Kathy went to her laptop and did a quick search for self-defense classes near her. She was surprised when one result popped up at her local community center. *Who knew*, she thought as she clicked the link. A website for 'Harding's Self Defense' and the instructor's name was Kyle Harding. She scrolled through the description and finally found the contact information at the bottom. She jotted down the number and when the class met on Saturdays.

"Uh-huh," a voice said behind her. Kathy turned around to find Stacey in the doorway with a grin. "I didn't mean to break your concentration, but the food is here."

"Be right there," she said grabbing the note she made about the class.

As Kathy walked to the dining room, she noticed a huge

blank space on Stacey's collage.

"What's going on here?" she said pointing to the blank space behind Stacey.

"Time for a change is all," she replied opening the box that contained the eggrolls. "So did you get a hold of your dad?" Kathy grabbed the chicken fried rice.

"Yeah, I did, but..."

"What?"

"I don't know. There was just something in his voice that didn't sound right."

"He's probably just trying to get used to being in the house by himself," Stacey assured her, "don't worry about it."

"Maybe you're right. Anyway, there's something I want to run by you," she said taking a bite of her fried rice.

"Sounds intriguing, what?"

"Yesterday, when I was out with Michael, he mentioned that I should think about taking a self-defense class."

"Really?" Stacey interrupted, "You mean he didn't volunteer to be your personal shadow," she teased.

Kathy rolled her eyes, "Shut up. Anyway, I was going to ask if you wanted to come with me next Saturday and check it out."

"Saturday, huh?" she said grabbing a napkin.

"They meet at the community center from 11 AM to 1 PM, and the instructor's name is Kyle Harding." Stacey thought about it for a minute.

"Sure, why not? It could be interesting."

"Maybe, you could use the experience for an article or something," Kathy hinted.

Stacey grinned, "We'll see, and what does this Kyle look like?" Kathy laughed.

"How did I know that would be your first thought."

"It could be important," Stacey protested with a smile.

"The website said it's an eight-week program, and the cost is $200." she replied finishing the last bit of rice on her plate. Stacey grabbed the fortunate cookies out of the take-out bag.

"Which one?" she asked holding one in each hand. Kathy looked at each one skeptically and finally picked the one on the right. She broke it open and took out the piece of paper. "What's it say?" Stacey asked impatiently.

"A good time to finish old tasks," Kathy read. "I wonder what that means?" Stacey shrugged her shoulders. "Okay, open yours."

"A smile is your personal welcome mat," Stacey read as they both giggled. "Well, you got the good one this time," she said tossing her away. "Anyway, I've got a few more paragraphs to write, pop in some quotes, and then, I send it in to see what the editor thinks," she said with satisfaction. Kathy cleared away the rest of the trash on the table.

"Not sure what I'll be doing tomorrow. Bailey hasn't said anything about a new client."

"Don't worry," Stacey replied flopping on the couch, "I'm sure there will be a shining new case for you as soon as you walk in." Kathy gave her a puzzled look.

"Who are you, Nostradamus?"

"Nope. Something better, a reporter with top-notch instincts." They both laughed as Kathy sat down on the couch beside her best friend.

"Ya know sometimes you are just so crazy."

"Not crazy, interesting. It's part of my charm," Stacey corrected as she turned on the TV.

"Ohh, is that what they're calling it these days?"

"Okay, we have two choices," Stacey said changing the subject, "option one is some survivor reality show, or option two the true crime channel."

"Let's see," Kathy said as she pretended to come to a decision, "true crime."

"That would be the right answer," Stacey said already going to that channel, "Ya know, some would say we watch too much of this stuff." Kathy grabbed a pillow and settled on the couch.

"Nah, no such thing."

"I would agree, but then I'm not the one who discovered a murder," she replied as the episode started. Kathy just nodded her head; she had almost forgotten about that; between spending the day with Michael and not having a case to take up her time, Kathy had accomplished her goal of distracting herself. Little did she know, however, that was going to be over when she walked into the office tomorrow.

Monday, April 21st

15

Kathy slowly turned over as her seven o'clock alarm started beeping. The true crime marathon went on longer than she had planned, so she was in no hurry this morning. Kathy turned off the alarm and picked up her locket as she rolled out of bed. She decided on a dark pair of jeans and a green dress shirt. She walked into the hallway and noticed that Stacey's bedroom door was still shut. *Some people have all the luck*, she thought, as she walked into the kitchen and poured herself a cup of coffee. She saw the blueberry muffins on the counter and picked up one just as her cell phone started to ring.

"Hello?" she said trying not to sound too sleepy.

"Did I catch you at a bad time?" Kathy was wide-awake now; it was Detective McMannis.

"No, no."

"Good. I need you to come down to the station for a few minutes."

"Anything wrong?" Kathy asked curiously.

"Just routine. I'm sure you know the way," he said sarcastically.

"I think I can find it," she shot back, "I'll be there in a few minutes," she said as he hung up. *He really needs to work on his people skills*, she thought, putting the cell back in her pocket. Kathy finished her muffin and poured herself another cup of coffee to go. It would definitely come in handy dealing with McMannis. As she picked up her bag, Kathy wondered what McMannis wanted to discuss. *Knowing him, anything was possible*, she thought as she headed out the door.

16

It was eight o'clock when Kathy pulled into the PD parking lot. She walked inside and noticed that it was busier than usual. Several people near the front desk were on their cell phones and two others, who were clearly lawyers, were shuffling through papers in their briefcases. She finally maneuvered her way to the front desk where Officer Garrison was trying to maintain order.

"Hello, Miss Kathy," he huffed.

"Hi, Garrison. I see you have a full house today."

"10-4 Miss Kathy. I presume you're looking for a certain cop."

Kathy shook her head, "No, this time I'm here to see Detective McMannis."

"Tough break," he replied as she walked to the elevators leaving Garrison to contend with the crowd at the desk.

She made the short trip to the third floor and made her way to McMannis' desk.

"Morning, detective. You wanted to see me," Kathy said as McMannis motioned for her to have a seat.

"Yes, I wanted to go over your statement you gave to the police," he said pulling out a piece of paper from the file in front of him.

"Anything wrong?" she asked as butterflies started to form in her stomach.

"You told Officer Richardson that you didn't see anybody the morning you went to meet the victim, is that correct?"

"Not that I remember. I walked in and called out to see if he was there. That's when I saw him against the column."

"Nobody else?"

"No, just Charlie and the blood," Kathy paused "Uh, detective, do they know exactly how Charlie died?"

McMannis folded his hands on the table, "M.E. said that there were two wounds. One to the abdomen and one to the throat, which was the one that really did him in. He eventually bled out.

Kathy swallowed her emotion, "Do you think he went quickly?"

"Don't know for sure. That wasn't in the report. The official cause of death was homicide by exsanguination."
Kathy silently nodded and suddenly realized that Reynolds wasn't around.

"Where's your partner?"

McMannis closed the file in front of him, "He's checking up on something."

"That something wouldn't happen to be a suspect, would it?" she prodded.

"It's too soon to tell. We've just started our investigation, so details are limited."

"Oh," she said nodding her head. "Is that it?" she asked as she started to leave.

"Our more thing," he said as Kathy sat back down. "The D. A. wanted me to give you this," he said handing her a piece of paper.

"What's this?"

"A subpoena," he said as Kathy just stared at him.

"Why?"

"The D. A. has his reasons. I'm just the messenger since I was meeting you anyway."

"The D. A. wouldn't be Phillips, would it?"

"Afraid so."

"Just great."

"If it's any consolation, I personally don't like him myself either, but his percentage of cases won is one of the highest. So, he's here to stay."

"Yeah, that doesn't help but thanks. Is that all?"

"Uh-huh." he said as Kathy started to get up, "Nice to see you again."

"Oh yeah, McMannis, a true pleasure," she said mockingly as she walked back to the elevators unaware of the small smile that crept onto the detective's face.

Kathy made the short trip back to the lobby where Officer Garrison still had his hands full. She pulled out her cell and texted Michael to meet her at Delany's for lunch. It was a moment or two before he sent back a reply confirming he would be there, if he could bring Jamie. Kathy quickly agreed, and they decided to meet in twenty minutes. She put her cell back in her pocket and walked out of the police station. *Why was McMannis acting so different?* she thought as she got into her car, *and where was Reynolds?* Kathy had always seen them together. Something was going on; they had found something or someone. The real question was who was that somebody.

17

Kathy pulled into the parking lot next to the Rosemont patrol car that was already there. Kathy saw Michael in the passenger side and smiled as they all got out. There was a nice breeze and not a cloud in the sky. She waited as Michael and Jamie met her at the door.

"Can we be of assistance?" Michael asked with a smile.

"I sure hope so," Kathy said grinning, "my morning has not gotten off to a good start."

"Well, Delany's is the best place to fix it," Jamie replied as he held the door as Kathy went in followed closely by his partner.

As they walked inside, they could hear the familiar sounds of Celtic rock flowing throughout the pub. Sam saw them as they came in and came over to seat them.

"Hey, Sam," Kathy said with a smile, "how are you?"

"I'm doing better," Sam replied as she showed them to a booth and they took a seat, "Ya know, one day at a time."

"You look good," Kathy replied taking the menu Sam handed her.

"Thanks," she said, "Kevin won't let me out of his sight."

"Smart," Jamie replied as Michael nodded in agreement.

"There ya go," Kathy replied, "you have certified approval."

Sam grinned as she shook her head, "What can I get you?" Kathy selected the chicken tenders with fries while the boys both picked a double cheeseburger. Sam took the menus and walked back to the kitchen.

"So, what's going on?" Michael asked.

Kathy huffed, "I had to see McMannis this morning."

"You have our sympathies," Jamie replied as Sam set their drinks on the table and went back to the bar.

"What did he want?" Michael asked.

"He said he needed to go over my statement, but it seemed, to me, like he was fishing for something," Kathy said as she took a sip of her drink.

"Wouldn't surprise me," Jamie replied.

"There wasn't anything suspicious in my statement, was there?"

"Kathy, it seemed straightforward to me," Michael reassured her as Sam brought their plates.

"Need anything else?" Sam asked.

"I don't think so," Kathy said eyeing the bar, "you better

get back to the bar before Kevin sends out a search," she said grinning.

"I know right, but he really has been sweet through the whole thing," she said looking back over her shoulder. "Well, ya'll enjoy," she said as she walked off.

"Like Michael said there weren't any red flags in your statement," Jamie said returning to the original topic.

"I hope you guys are right; and to top it off, he handed me a subpoena." Michael and Jamie stopped eating.

"Damn," Michael said, "well, don't worry. It's probably routine. I mean you were the one who found the body," he added trying to wipe the worried look off her face.

"Copy that. The D.A. is probably looking for a star witness," Jamie added with a smile.

"It will not be me," Kathy said adamantly.

"Now how do you know unless you give him a chance?" Michael teased.

"I agree with Officer Winters; there could be a sparking personality underneath that exterior," Jamie added as he finished his burger.

"Well, aren't you both just full of advice," Kathy replied as she threw a balled up napkin at Michael.

"All part of the job," Jamie said as his walkie-talkie started to crackle.

'Calling all available units please respond to a 10-52 at 1306 Bridge Street. Domestic disturbance in progress, requesting 10-85. One female and two males'

'Copy that dispatch. 243 PC Richardson and PC Winters responding.'

'Copy 243. Possible weapons on scene.'

'Copy dispatch. We're en route.'

'Copy 243. Getting further information.'

'10-4 dispatch.' Jamie said as he took the radio and started for the car.

"Sorry," Michael said as he got out of the booth.

"I know, I know," Kathy said, "Duty calls." She got up and took the check from Michael. "I'll take care of this; you go save the day." Kathy flopped back down in the booth as the two officers hurried out of the pub.

"Emergency, huh?" Sam asked walking over.

"Yep," she replied handing Sam the check and her card.

"Well, look at it this way. At least he has a good reason for leaving."

"I know, you're right. It's just so abrupt. Anyway, I guess I have some work that needs my attention. Thanks, Sam," she said as she followed Sam to the bar to pay the bill.

As Kathy walked outside and felt inside her bag for her phone; she inadvertently pulled out the note instead. As she looked at it, she couldn't shake the unsettled feeling it gave her. She decided to go to the office to see if she could make any sense of it.

18

It was one o'clock when Kathy walked into the office. She waved to Sally, who was in the middle of a phone conversation and headed down the hallway to her office. Kathy walked inside and closed the door behind her. She sat down behind her desk and laid the note on top.

'No good deed goes unpunished.'

-W

Kathy re-read the message staring at her. *What does that mean?*, she thought to herself. Kathy looked at the note, a white piece of paper, written in pen, and signed 'W'. Kathy took a legal pad from the top drawer of her desk and the file she had from the Chase Wagner case. She flipped through her notes until she came to the section on i guardiani.

"Well, there's no 'W' in that word," Kathy remarked as

she booted up her laptop. She opened up Google and typed 'i guardiani' in the search box. "Let's see what we've got," she said as the results came up. "Ok, so i guardiani is Italian for the gatekeepers. That sounds ominous," she said as she clicked the news tab and scrolled through the results. The first two pages were nothing but Italian news headlines, but then she saw one that caught her eye.

I guardiani: a family business or international crime syndicate. "Now we're talking," she said as she clicked on the link. A news article slowly appeared on the screen as she began to scan the article. The article seemed to suggest that the business known as 'i guardiani' was more than just a family business. With assets in the millions and contacts all over the world, i guardiani was on the list of every crime taskforce, only there was never enough evidence for charges to stick. Kathy made some more notes, then returned to her note still lying on the desk. Kathy wondered if the note and the i guardiani were connected.

Thoroughly stumped Kathy glanced around the office and noticed that she hadn't put her new books on the shelf yet. She took the two bags sitting on the floor and carefully took the titles out and placed them neatly on the shelf. As she looked at the row of books, she hoped that she would become a great investigator. "Maybe, one day," she sighed as she threw the empty bags in the trash. She went back over to her desk and put the note back in her bag. She saw the subpoena that McMannis had so graciously bestowed upon her crammed in her bag, and decided to make a quick call. She quickly dialed Bailey's number, but it went straight to voicemail.

"Hey Bailey, it's Kathy. I just wanted to let you know that I got a subpoena from McMannis this morning. Just wanted your thoughts about it. Talk to you later." Kathy hung up and decided to go back to the apartment. She cleaned up her dead-end leads, grabbed her bag, and walked out of her office. She smiled as she saw the silver lettering on the door that read Kathy Hamilton, Investigator. She walked down the hallway, a little defeated, and saw Sally at the desk.

"Done for the day?" Sally asked as Kathy leaned on the desk.

"I think so."

"You don't sound too sure."

"No," Kathy sighed. "Just thinking, but I'm not getting anywhere."

"I'd love to help, but I'll leave that to the professionals," she said with a wink.

"Professional," Kathy repeated. "I sure hope so."

"See ya tomorrow," Sally said as Kathy waved goodbye. Kathy walked into a cool breeze and took a deep breath. She wished she was a professional, but right now she had to see a certain reporter. Two heads were always better than one, or at least she hoped so, as she got into her car and pulled out of the parking lot.

19

It was a little after five o'clock when Kathy walked into the apartment. She had stopped to pick up some subs for supper and also to gain the input of a certain reporter.

"Hey Stace, you here?" she called out as she closed the door behind her.

"I am now," Stacey replied turning in her chair as Kathy came into view.

"I see you're hard at work," she commented as she laid the sub on the table and took a seat.

"When am I not?" she replied with a wink. "Actually, I'm catching up on my emails, but still...hard at work."

Kathy giggled, "You're a trip."

"What's that on the table?" she said finally noticing the subs.

"I thought we could eat while I get your input on some things that happened today," Kathy said noticing the gleam in her friend's eye.

"Sounds interesting but...," she paused "what kind of sub?"

"Ham and cheese for me, and there might be a spicy Italian for somebody."

"I will gladly take it off your hands," she said as she quickly moved from the desk to the kitchen table. "So, what's on your mind?" she asked as she slid the sub over and grabbed a napkin. Kathy grinned as she grabbed two bottles of water from the fridge and sat down.

"Well, this morning I get a call from Detective McMannis."

"Wait a minute," Stacey interrupted. "Any conversation that starts with him can't be good."

"He said he needed to talk to me about my statement I gave, and we did, but before I left he handed me a subpoena."

Stacey raised her eyebrows, "a what?"

"You heard me."

"How thoughtful!"

"Wasn't it. Anyway, I talked to Michael and Jamie about it, and they both said my statement was fine."

"Ah yes, the dream team," Stacey sighed. "How is that blond hair blue-eyed dreamboat?"

Kathy rolled her eyes, "Can we focus please?"

"Trust me, I am," Stacey replied with a grin.

"On my situation," she said trying not to laugh.

"Fine, fine. For what it's worth, I think they're right. I wouldn't stress about it. Probably routine," she said taking a sip of her bottled water.

"I hope so. I also asked him what the M.E. said about Charlie's cause of death."

"And?"

"He said that there were two wounds, one to the throat and one to the abdomen. He didn't really elaborate more than that."

"Well, at least he probably went fast."

"I hope so. I hate to think Charlie died a horrible death just because I didn't answer my phone," Kathy said as a small tear ran down her cheek.

"Stop it," Stacey said flatly. "None of this is your fault. Not one bit. Whoever killed Charlie should be the one crying and feeling sorry."

Kathy took a deep breath, "Thanks. You're right."

"Of course, I'm right," Stacey said as Kathy shook her head. Her best friend always knew how to cheer her up.

"You know, I've been thinking a lot about Charlie."

"Kathy, what did I just say?"

"No. I mean, why Charlie?" Stacey slid the sub aside.

"You're gonna have to be more specific than that?"

"Why kill Charlie? Is it because of what he knew or saw? Why go to such lengths to silence him?"

"Okay, I think I see where you're going."

"It just feels like there's something else going on here?"

"Have anything in mind?"

"Possibly," Kathy said then paused.

"Well, don't leave me in suspense."

"I've been looking at the Chase Wagner case and..."

"I thought they found him not guilty."

"I'm not talking about him. In my notes, I came across an article about an organization called 'i guardiani'. And I was just considering the possibility that there might be a connection to Charlie," Kathy finally said.

"Hmmm. Well, if there is a connection, you're going to have a hell of a time proving it."

"Not the rousing support I was expecting."

"I'm just saying, take it from someone who knows; you are going to have to have solid evidence for something like this," Kathy threw her head back and exhaled. "So, let me know how I can help." Kathy popped her head back up.

"That sounds like the reporter I know."

"I have an idea. Why don't you go back to the PD and see what McMannis thinks?"

"What?"

"Now, wait a minute. You don't have to tell him everything. Just throw a little out there and see what sticks. I'm sure it's what he does all the time."

"I guess doing something is better than nothing."

"Sounds like a winning attitude to me. Where did you pick it up from?"

Kathy shrugged her shoulders, "Oh, some reporter I know." They both laughed.

"Let's clean this mess away, and then, I've got to get back to my email cleaning."

Kathy and Stacey cleaned off the table and Stacey went back to her desk. Kathy went to her room and flopped down on the bed. She was not looking forward to talking to Detective McMannis again. *And where was Detective Reynolds?* Kathy wondered. Kathy had so many questions; she hoped tomorrow, she'd finally get some answers.

Tuesday, April 22nd

20

Kathy had hoped that a good night's rest would put her in the right frame of mind, but all the questions rolling around in her head prevented all hopes of any rest. She eventually rolled out of bed and clasped her necklace around her neck. She pulled on a dark pair of jeans and a dark grey cold-shoulder top.

Kathy walked into the kitchen and saw a pink post-it on the coffeepot. It was from Stacey letting her know that she had already left to talk to her editor at the Rosemont Observer.

I must be too predictable, Kathy thought as she tossed the note away and poured herself a cup of coffee. She inhaled the aroma and checked the clock on her phone. *McMannis should be in by now*, she thought to herself. She grabbed her bag from the couch in the living room and threw it on her shoulder. Something told her that she was not going to like what McMannis had to say about her theory.

21

Kathy walked into the Rosemont PD and immediately noticed that it was unusually calm. Except for a few phones ringing, there was no chaotic scene at the front desk. She waved hello to Garrison, who was smiling for a change and made that short trip to the third floor.

She stepped off the elevator and suddenly felt a little nervous. As McMannis' desk came into view, she saw him sitting looking at a case board. *Well, here goes nothing*, she thought as he finally saw her coming toward him.

"Miss Kathy, what can I do for you this time?" he said and pointed to a chair as she took a seat.

"I had a theory about Charlie, and I wanted to run it by you."

"Really?" he said mildly intrigued.

"Yes, I was thinking about why somebody would go to such lengths to silence someone like Charlie."

"So, you've been thinking about murder suspects for Charlie's death," he interrupted.

"Umm, more or less," she replied hesitantly.

"I believe I can save you the trouble," he said with a smile.

"What do you mean?"

"We already have a suspect for the murder of Charlie Goldson."

"Really?"

"As soon as Reynolds gets back, we are going to pick him up."

"Uh-huh. I assume you have substantial evidence," Kathy replied.

"I think that lawyer is starting to rub off on you, Miss Kathy," he said amused. "Yes, we do. Why the interest?"

"It's personal since I was the one who found Charlie," Kathy stated flatly.

"Yes, you did," the detective replied leaning back in his chair. "Anything else I can help you with? What about this theory you have?" he asked only half-serious.

"Never mind. I won't take up any more of your time," Kathy said as she got up to leave when McMannis added.

"Oh, before you leave, I had two patrol officers pay me a visit yesterday." Kathy turned around.

"Interesting."

"Uh-huh. I found it interesting that they felt the need to reiterate how solid your statement was."

"I'm sure they were just trying to be helpful. I know how much you hate chasing down bad leads," Kathy shot back as she turned around and left Detective McMannis standing there. She wasn't sure if she was embarrassed or upset. She pressed the button for the elevator and impatiently waited. She finally heard the ding and started to step on when she walked right into Commander Winters.

"Good morning, Mr. Winters," Kathy said with a smile.

"Good morning. What brings you down to the PD this morning?" he said as he stepped off the elevator. "You're on the wrong floor if you're looking for Officer Winters."

Kathy smiled, "Oh no, I just had an errand to run."

"Nothing serious?"

"Kathy shook her head no, "Just tying up loose ends."

"Good to hear. Say hello to your dad for me. It was nice seeing him."

"Oh, you saw dad?" Kathy asked surprised.

"Only for a moment," he recovered. "Well, I have an appointment to get to. It was nice seeing you, Kathy."

"You too, Mr. Winters," she said as she watched him walk away.

Kathy pressed the elevator button again and stepped on. Her dad hadn't mentioned seeing Commander Winters. She wondered what that was about; it was just not like him. It was probably nothing though; they were all close since Mom's case. Kathy pushed it from her mind and re-focused on what Detective McMannis had just told her. Kathy's mind began to wonder who this suspect could be and what his connection could be to Charlie.

22

McMannis was savoring the last of his morning coffee. It wasn't exactly Starbucks, but at least it wasn't burnt either. He took the last sip when Detective Austin came over and took a seat on his desk.

"The guys wanted to know how Parker is doing." McMannis didn't take his eyes off his case board.

"He's a trooper, as usual. I've got some time coming. I'll probably check in on him and see how he's holding up," he said unknowingly rubbing his left shoulder.

"Just let him know that he's still one of us. We're all still thinking about him," Detective Austin said as he slapped McMannis on the back and returned to his desk. McMannis tried not to dwell too long on Detective Parker; it never ended well. But it was his duty to check in with him. He owed him at least that much.

As McMannis sat his styrofoam cup down, he browsed through the file of their suspect. *Reynolds should be back soon*, he thought glancing at the station wall clock. He was about to pick up the phone when he saw his long-awaited partner walking in his direction.

"So, you decided to come back after all," McMannis jabbed.

"Why, did you miss me?" Reynolds asked throwing his coat on the back of his chair and taking a seat.

"Yeah, about as much as my last ex-wife," McMannis retorted. "So, how's the suspect?"

"Tucked safely away in a cell. He kept shouting that he wanted his stuff back."

"Really?"

"Yeah, and he had a visitor before I left."

"Do tell."

"Bailey Clark," Reynolds replied as McMannis leaned toward him.

"What did he want?"

"He's going to represent him and somehow persuaded the guards to let our suspect keep a picture."

"Sentimental, is he?"

"Who cares. It made him stop yelling. Anyway, since Bailey is involved now, we should be getting a visit from our favorite female investigator," Reynolds hinted with a smile.

"Actually, she was just here."

"So soon. Damn, she's fast."

"I called her. The D. A. had a subpoena for her and since I had to talk to her anyway, I delivered it. Then, she came back today with some questions, but I deflected."

"Oh," Reynolds said deflated.

"Problem?"

"Nah, I'm just sorry I missed the encounter. She always puts you such in a wonderful disposition."

"Can it, Reynolds."

"I would've liked to have seen her."

"Don't," McMannis warned.

"What?"

"She works for the other side, so don't get attached. Remember, you're married."

"It's not like that," Reynolds replied. "Don't you have female friends?" McMannis shot him a hard look. "Right, I forgot. You married all of yours, but admit it, she's nice to be around."

"I don't know about that but, she's not all bad," he said as he returned to the case file on his desk.

23

It was almost eleven when Kathy pulled into AmiLee's Cafe's parking lot. AmiLee's was a small cafe where you could grab a salad, soup, or a sandwich if you wanted something more substantial. With its hardwood floors, white walls, small cafe tables, and vintage art décor, it was such a cozy place to stop in and grab a bite. Kathy's favorite part was the natural lighting, which she thought, set everything off just right.

Kathy walked in and sat down at one of the tables by a window. She picked up the menu when she heard someone call her name.

"Kathy!" She turned around and saw Brianna coming toward her.

"Hey, Bri!" she said as her friend came over to her table.

"Saving this seat for anyone?"

"Uh-huh, for you," Kathy said smiling as the waitress came over.

"You two ready to order?" a slim, blonde woman asked.

"Yes," Kathy replied. "I'll have a Caesar salad with grilled chicken and water."

"And you?" the waitress asked turning toward Brianna.

"I think I'll have the broccoli and cheese soup with an iced coffee."

"Okay, I'll be back," she said as she turned and headed toward the kitchen.

"So, what's new with you?" Brianna asked once the waitress was out of earshot.

"I've been officially hired by Bailey Clark as an investigator."

"Very nice. What you've always wanted."

"That's true, but sometimes I wish I was better at it," Kathy confessed.

"Don't worry, you were born to do this. Trust me."

"Thanks," Kathy said as the waitress brought their orders.

"Let me know if you need anything else," she said as she walked away.

"So, what about you?" Kathy said picking up her fork.

"Well, actually I have some exciting news," Brianna said crumpling a cracker into her soup.

"Let's hear it."

"I have my first art exhibit this Sunday at the gallery," she said beaming.

"Brianna, that's amazing! What's the exhibit?"

"It's a collection of pieces with a local representation theme. It's not as impressive as some of the other exhibits, but at least I've got my foot in the door, right?"

"I have no doubt that your exhibit will be the talk of the show," Kathy said remembering the salad in front of her.

"So, I was wondering if you would like to be a part of my moral support?"

Kathy paused for a moment, "Only if I can bring a few friends with me," she said with a smile.

"That would be perfect," Brianna replied as she took a sip of her soup.

"What time is the big event?"

"It is this Sunday at The Rose Art Gallery from two to six p.m."

"Got it," Kathy replied as she added the event to the calendar on her cell. "We will definitely be there."

"I can't tell if I'm excited or nervous. I think this is my chance to really get noticed."

"Oh, you will. Maybe you'll have better luck than me right now."

"Uh-oh, that doesn't sound good."

"No, I mean I'm just at a brick wall and I'm not sure how to get through it or over it," Kathy confessed as she took another bite of her salad.

"I'm sure you can handle it. You always do," her friend assured her as her phone rang. "Oh, it's the gallery. I've got to run," she said grabbing her purse. "Nice to see you Kathy, and don't worry, I'm sure you'll figure it out," she said as she quickly flagged down the waitress for her check. Kathy waved goodbye as her friend left the cafe. She hoped Brianna was right, but right now all she had was puzzles with no clues in sight.

24

It was two o'clock when Kathy walked into the office. She found Sally behind the desk, but for a change, she wasn't on the phone.

"Hey, Sally, what'cha got there?" Kathy asked propping her arms on the reception desk.

"Just the mail," Sally sighed. "Bills, advertisements, and oh what's this? More advertisements." Kathy gave a small smile at Sally's mocked expression.

"Is Bailey in?"

"He is, and he told me to tell you to drop by when you came in."

"Anything wrong?"

"Just delivering the message," Sally said flipping through the pieces of mail.

"Okay, thanks Sally," she said as she walked down the hallway and knocked on Bailey's door.

"Come on in," Bailey said as Kathy walked in and took a seat.

"Sally said you wanted to see me," Kathy said noticing that Vicky was not around.

"I did," Bailey replied opening a file lying on his desk. "Vicky was at the courthouse on her normal run, and she stumbled on an interesting piece of information."

"What's that?"

"It seems the police have arrested a suspect for the Charles Goldson murder."

"Really," Kathy replied trying to seem genuine.

"Now, the court was going to appoint an attorney for this person, but after Vicky called me and informed me on what was going on, I have decided to take this client pro bono."

"Why's that?"

"Two reasons. One, because given the present situation of this client he could never afford the services of a decent lawyer and two, probably most importantly, I feel uneasy about not finding Charlie, and so, I am evening out the scales."

"I see."

"This is in no way a reflection on you, Kathy," he emphasized. "I just think this is something I need to do."

"I agree," Kathy cut in. "I know everyone keeps telling me that it's not my fault, but I do feel guilty about Charlie. So, I'm all in."

“Excellent,” he said smiling. “Kathy, meet our new client, Simon,” he said handing Kathy a file.

“Kind of thin, isn’t it?” she replied as she looked at it skeptically.

“Unfortunately, yes,” Bailey sighed. “So, it’s going to be up to you to fill in the holes. All that we know about our client, for the present, is that his name is Simon and he’s been living on the streets for several years. There’s no record of medical history or family. So, you’ve got your work cut out for you this time.”

“Where do you want me to start?” Kathy replied with determination.

“First, go through the file. What little there is in it. Then, get as much background on our client as possible. See if there are any witnesses and then pay a visit to Charlie’s family.”

Kathy’s eyebrows shot up, “Charlie’s what?”

“He has a wife living in town and one daughter. Just see what you can get out of them.” Kathy couldn’t believe her ears. Charlie had a family.

“Okay, I’m on it,” she replied as she picked up her bag and walked across the hallway to her office to get started.

25

Simon stared at the light flickering overhead. He lay on the cot in his cell and tried to make sense of what was happening. The memories that played over and over in his mind, seemed more like scenes from a movie than flashes of his own life. Simon laid there, in the orange jumpsuit that was given to him when he was processed, and slowly turned over on his side. He remembered finding his shiv under his mat, but it was dirty. He remembered taking it outside to clean it, then those men took him away and put him in here. *I didn't do anything wrong*, he thought to himself, *I just want to be left alone*. Simon took the photo out of his pocket; it was the only thing that lawyer had persuaded them to let him keep. He traced his fingers over the outlines of the two faces in the picture. He wished he could tell them the truth, but it was too painful. They wouldn't understand, he didn't understand.

Why did I think that I could just run away? I can't go back; too much has happened, he thought regrettably. Simon clenched his eyes shut; his head was hurting again. "Ugh," he moaned. The headaches were getting worse, just like the doctor said they would. *Why can't it just be over?*, he thought to himself. Simon got up and cradled his head in his hands; he needed help.

"Hey, someone!" he called out. "I need help! Please, help me!" A prison guard casually walked over to his cell.

"What now?" he barked.

"Please, I need some medicine. My head hurts," he pleaded. The prison guard grabbed his walkie talkie from his belt.

"Hey, Tim, I need to take 4C to the medic. Mind covering for me?"

"Be there in five," the voice replied.

"Okay you," the guard said signaling for Simon's cell to be opened. "Let's go." Simon stood there as the guard placed him in handcuffs and slowly walked him out.

26

Kathy closed the door behind her, sat down at her desk, and lay the file on top. "Alright," she said opening the file. "Let's see what we've got." She found the M.E. report and slowly went over it. "Time of death was between eight p.m. and twelve a.m. One wound to the throat and the second to the abdomen. On closer examination, during the autopsy, it was found that the laceration to the throat severed one of the carotid arteries which explains the amount the blood loss of the victim." Kathy took a deep breath, "Charlie what happened to you?" she asked as she flipped the page. "Multiple bruises to the face, but no defensive marks were found. The cause of death was homicide by exsanguination."

Kathy got up from the desk and pulled the case board over. She grabbed a dry erase marker to start a timeline. "Okay, so from eight p.m. to twelve a.m. as my window, and let's say two hours before that," Kathy sighed. "Yeah, not asking too much at all." She went back to the file and flipped to the pages on the suspect or, Kathy corrected herself, the new client. "So, who is our new client?" she asked skimming over the information. "Calls himself Simon, brown hair, brown eyes, five-foot-seven, and thirty-one years old. Kind of young to be living on the streets," she commented as she continued on. "Fingerprint match still pending and no criminal history." Kathy made a few notes, and then, went to the section on the crime scene, not that she needed much help with that. It was still clear in her mind; she shook it off and re-focused on the report in front of her. "Murder weapon is a shiv composed of a metal blade wrapped in duct tape wrapped multiple times around the bottom to form a handle. It was found on the suspect when he was taken into custody. The blood found on the weapon is a match to the blood type of the victim. "Well, that's not good," Kathy remarked as she continued reading. "Blood spatter was found on the ground where the victim's body was found."

Kathy looked at the crime scene photos and then remembered something. She pulled out her cell phone and went to the photo gallery. There they were, the photos she took before the police got there. Kathy loaded them onto her laptop and printed them out. She pinned them onto the case board once the printer finally decided to spit them out. She stood back to evaluate her progress. "Well, at last, it looks like I'm getting somewhere," she sighed and went back to the file. The first person on her witness list was Charlie's wife, Claire Schofield. "Huh, I wonder why she went back to her maiden name?"

Kathy wrote down the address in her notebook and decided to try a longshot. *Everybody has a family,* she thought to herself as she went to her laptop and pulled up the missing persons database. She typed in her information into the search fields, said a quick prayer, and clicked the search button. She waited impatiently as the database combed through all the records until finally, a search results page popped up. Kathy carefully looked at each result, and then, one caught Kathy's eye. The face in the picture was more clean-cut and looked a little younger, but that was Simon. Kathy looked at the information beside the picture. Hair and eyes were the same, and the date of birth matched Simon's present age. Kathy looked below at the contact information, which listed Darren and Haley Bradwell from Pennsylvania. Their client's name was Simon Bradwell, and he had been missing for several years. Kathy wrote down the contact number listed and put a star beside it to make sure that was one of the things she told Bailey in her case update. She glanced at the clock on her phone which read four o'clock and decided to make a quick stop by the crime scene before heading to the apartment. Kathy carefully put the case file back in order and shut down her laptop. *Who knows*, she thought to herself, *maybe I'll stumble on something useful.*

27

Kathy's trailblazer came to a slow stop as the crime scene came into view. The yellow police tape was still there along with two cops watching over the area. Kathy clipped her ID badge on, grabbed her bag, and slowly made her way to the crime scene. As she came closer, one of the cops met her at the tape.

"My name is Kathy Hamilton. I'm an investigator with Bailey Clark, just wanted to take another look guys." The two cops looked at each other, then, one officer handed her a clipboard to sign. Kathy carefully logged in and handed the clipboard back.

"Alright, go on in," he said holding the police tape up as Kathy ducked under. "Just remember, don't touch anything," he added as Kathy walked past him.

"I got it, officer. No touching at all," Kathy assured

him as she turned her attention to the scene in front of her. As Kathy walked inside, she tried to push the memories of what she had seen earlier away, but she wasn't having much luck. Kathy stopped as she stood in exactly the same spot when she found Charlie. She knew she shouldn't get emotionally involved, but she couldn't help it.

"Oh, Charlie. I'm so sorry," she whispered as she wiped a tear from her cheek. "I will find out what happened to you," she promised and took out her notepad. "So, the report said that you had no defensive wounds. Why was that Charlie?" Kathy mused the thought over as she began to slowly scan the area. "Were you tied up, unconscious, or both?" Kathy looked back in her notes and read that some of the bruises were on Charlie's wrists. "Hmm, but no restraints were found." Kathy walked closer to the column where she found Charlie taking care to stay away from the bloodstains still visible on the ground. She took a pen from her bag and carefully used it to search through the dirt around the column. "C'mon Charlie. Help me out," she breathed. She slowly moved the dirt around until Kathy thought she saw something. She used the pen to move it away from the beam. "What is this?" she whispered as she pushed it into full view. A piece of clear plastic, no more than, maybe, a quarter of an inch long. Kathy pulled out her cell phone and snapped a quick picture then took a small plastic baggie from her bag. She had found a crime scene equipment checklist in one of her books, and she had made sure that she had checked off every single item. Kathy carefully took her tweezers, placed the plastic in the bag, and slipped it into her bag. Kathy got up and looked around; the police had taken most of Charlie's and Simon's things for evidence, but the outlines were still there. "So, Charlie and Simon lived in close proximity to each other most of the time. So, what was the difference this time?" she whispered as she looked around for clues. There was easy access to Simon's things. *No security systems here, unless the pigeons count,* Kathy mused, smiling to herself. "So, Simon slept in this corner, and Charlie was directly opposite, but..." Kathy stopped and walked over to a third corner, "...who slept here?" There was a faint outline of a sleeping bag, some crumpled-up newspapers, and one empty food can. Kathy took the baggie that contained the plastic she had found and taken another look at it. "You mean something, don't you?" Kathy quickly jotted down her observations and then gave Bailey a call.

"Bailey Clark."

"Hi Bailey, it's Kathy."

"It's after five, so I'm assuming, you have something."

"Not sure. I went back to the crime scene to take another look, and Bailey, I found something."

"What exactly?" he said with growing interest.

"It's just a small piece of plastic, but I found it at the column where Charlie was found."

"Uh-huh."

"Yeah, so I put it in a baggie and thought I'd give you a call."

"Okay. I'm going to give the D. A. a call and make sure we're all clear on this. You hand it to the cops stationed out front, and we'll proceed from there."

"Okay."

"But before you do," Bailey quickly added. "What's your initial observation about it?" Kathy turned the baggie over in her hand.

"Well, Bailey, it's pretty small but it sort of looks like..."

"Like what?"

"Like a piece of a plastic tie."

"Huh. Are you sure?"

"Like I said, it's small, but you asked for my observation and that's it."

"Alright."

"You know, in the police report, it said that Charlie had bruises around his wrists. Could the bruises have been made by plastic ties?"

"An excellent question. I don't know but it's possible and as a defense attorney I live in the realm of possibility. So, I'll think about it and we'll see where it goes."

"Whatever you say, Bailey."

"I'll see you tomorrow, and good work Miss Hamilton."

"Thanks, Bailey, I'll update you tomorrow on the rest."

"Sounds good," he said and hung up.

Kathy put her notepad back in her bag when the bloodstains caught her eye, again. Charlie's message was still faintly visible, I saw him. *Of all things to write, why that?* Kathy wondered. Was he talking about who killed him or was he referring to the Chase Wagner case? Kathy shook her head as her phone vibrated. She took it out and saw that Stacey had sent her a text. She texted back that she would be back soon and yes, pizza was fine for dinner. She put her phone back in her pocket and started to walk out, but she couldn't. She turned back around and there was Charlie, lying on the ground, covered in blood. Kathy closed her eyes and took a deep breath. When she opened her eyes, Charlie was gone and only the bloodstain remained. Kathy put away her notepad and looked at the baggie in her hand, "I know I can't prove it now, but I will. This plastic was used to hold you somehow," she tightened her grip on the bag. "I will prove it Charlie. I will find the truth."

28

Reynolds sat at his desk in amusement as he watched his partner, for the second time, rifle through his wallet.

"Should we call out the National Guard? he jabbed.

"We might have to if I don't find that damn dry cleaning receipt," Detective McMannis replied clearly frustrated.

"Would this be a bad time to talk about your need for organization?" Reynolds asked smiling. McMannis ignored him, put his wallet back, and began searching in his coat pockets.

"Ha! Got it," he said triumphantly.

"I never knew you were so concerned over your dry-cleaning."

"Usually no, but this is for my court suit. We have to look our best for the department you know."

"You mean they won't take you the way you are?"

Reynolds asked feigning surprise.

"Can we get back to the case?"

"Yes, boss. The blood match on the murder weapon is a match to our victim. We just got a fingerprint match on our suspect. We had to search out of state, but the prints do match the ones on our murder weapon. We are still waiting on the results from the evidence turned over by the defense."

"Good. Tell the lab to keep it up and let us know when they have something."

"10-4," Reynolds said making a note of it.

"Oh, and I heard that the D. A. wants a doctor to analyze our suspect."

"I can only imagine how that will go," McMannis commented as he noticed someone in the corner of his eye. "Damn."

"What now?"

"The captain is coming. Get ready."

"Not me, you do the talking," Reynolds said straightening up his desk. Captain Thomas walked directly toward their case board.

"So, what progress is there on the case?"

McMannis cleared his throat, "We've got a print match on the murder weapon to our suspect and the M.E. is certain that our murder weapon is what was used on our VIC. We're still waiting on the piece of evidence that the defense turned over."

"Any loose ends?"

"No sir, all our evidence points to our suspect."

"Good to hear," Captain Thomas nodded his approval. "Oh, I hear you'll be testifying in court on this case."

"Yes, sir, the suit is all ready to go."

"Good job detective. Make the department look good," the captain replied as Reynolds stifled a laugh. "Anything wrong, Reynolds?"

"No, sir. Just got choked."

"Uh-huh. Good work the both of you," he said as he moved on to the next detectives on his rounds. Reynolds looked at McMannis and couldn't help but grin.

"Not one word, Reynolds," McMannis warned. "Not one word."

29

It was six-thirty in the evenig when Kathy walked through her apartment door, and she was grateful that Stacey had already ordered dinner.

"Hey, I'm here!" she called out.

"About time," Stacey replied as her roommate walked into the kitchen and put her bag on the table.

"Wow! That looks so good," she said grabbing a plate.

"Tough day?"

"Yes and no."

"Thanks for clearing that up."

"No, I mean I had to go back to the crime scene and...."

"Uh-huh. I got it."

"Yeah," Kathy took a breath.

"Well?"

"Well, what?" Kathy said taking a bite of pizza.

"What happened?" Stacey asked exasperated.

Kathy smiled, "I wanted to sort out a few things in the police report."

"What? Did they leave something out?"

"No. They said that no restraints were found at the scene, but Charlie had bruises around his wrists."

"Maybe the killer took them with him?"

"Possibly and another thing, I was looking at the layout, and it looked like there was a third bed or living area. Simon and Charlie were opposite of each other, but there was no mention of a third person."

"Really?" Stacey said intrigued. "Maybe the killer?"

"Not sure, and I still have a few more witnesses to talk to. What have you been up to?"

"Me?" Stacey asked mockingly, "now, why would you think that?"

"Cough it up, Stace."

"Okay," she said as she grabbed her notepad off of her desk. "I've scheduled interviews with all the town council candidates, and I am now digging up all the dirt I can so I can do a thorough job. You know, no stone unturned."

"Oh, yes. I know you're enjoying that part."

"This could be my moment to jump from the back page to the front page. I guess you could say that I'm nervously excited."

"So, this is you nervously excited?" Kathy said smiling.

"You look like you've drunk three pots of coffee."

"Actually, only one and a half."

"Good grief. I think I'll take my work to my room and work on my witness list there. You seem to have all you can handle."

"What do you mean? I am perfectly fine," Stacey replied as she nervously tapped her fingers on the table.

"Yeah, okay," Kathy said slinging her bag over her shoulder. "You keep digging away and I'll finish this in my room," she said taking her plate and drink. "And one more thing, Stacey please don't drink any more coffee."

"Yeah, you might be right."

"Yeah, see you in the morning."

"Uh-huh," Stacey said already back at her desk jotting down her thoughts in her notebook.

Kathy closed her bedroom door and sat her food on her desk. She took out her notepad and the police report and started making her witness list. "So, who's the first lucky person I get to talk to?" Kathy said as she looked over the statements. "It looks like it's you, Claire." Kathy wrote down the name Claire Schofield and put the name Goldson in parenthesis. Kathy went back and forth between police statements and cheese pizza until she came up with three more names: Alyssa Goldson, Charlie's daughter; Sophie Ramirez, the gas station attendant; and Lynn Tyler, the employee at Goodwill. "That looks like a good start," she said as she yawned. Kathy looked at the first name on her list, Claire Scholfield. *Why would she go back to her maiden name,* Kathy thought, *and why did Charlie leave?* Kathy put her notepad in her bag and got ready for bed. Tomorrow, she would get to the bottom of that story.

Wednesday, April 23rd

30

Kathy woke up, at seven a.m., to the ringing of her alarm clock. She fumbled for her cell and finally shut it off. She slowly got out of bed and threw on a pair of jeans and a lilac dress shirt. She clasped her necklace on and went to see about breakfast. As she walked into the kitchen, she found Stacey exactly where she had left her, writing at her desk.

"Don't tell me you were up all night," Kathy said grabbing a muffin off of the counter.

"No, don't be ridiculous. I took a small nap and then went back over my notes before my first candidate interview."

"Good grief," Kathy replied as she reached for the coffeepot.

"Hey, pour me one."

"Oh, no. I think you still have plenty of caffeine in your

system."

"Yes, mother," Stacey said with a grin.

"Yeah, well, you won't be smiling this afternoon when you crash."

"Reporters don't crash, they maneuver gracefully."

"Okay Miss graceful, I'll remember that for later," Kathy said checking the time. "Anyway, I gotta go. The office is waiting."

"Alright, see you later."

"See ya," Kathy said as she picked up her bag and walked out the door.

31

It was exactly eight when Kathy walked through the office door. She saw Sally at her usual place, behind the desk and on the phone.

"Hi, Sally."

"One moment, please. Uh, Kathy."

"What it is?"

"Bailey needs to see you in his office."

"Okay," Kathy replied as Sally returned to her phone conversation. Kathy walked down the hallway and knocked on Bailey's door.

"Come on in," Bailey's voice called out. Kathy walked in to find Bailey and Vicky waiting for her.

"Sally said you needed to see me."

"Take a seat, Kathy," he said pointing to the chair. "The

D.A. called this morning and confirmed that they will be calling you to testify at the trial tomorrow."

"Oh, great," Kathy said rolling her eyes.

"I believe he said that you are second on the list."

"Bailey, I don't do courtrooms. I'm much better in the field, ya know, investigating."

"Sorry but there's no way out," he said giving her a sympathetic look. "But Vicky is here to make sure it's as painless as possible."

"Well, I'm not a miracle worker. It is D.A. Phillips after all but I'll do my best. Don't worry Kathy. You're not a suspect, you're just background support."

"Sure, thanks."

"Before I go to the courthouse, do you have any information for me?" Bailey said organizing his briefcase.

"Actually, I found some information on our client."

Bailey stopped what he was doing, "Do tell."

"I did a search of Simon in the missing persons database, and I think I found a match." Bailey and Vicky both stared at her.

"Are you sure it's Simon?" Bailey said hopefully.

"I believe so. Same age, hair, and eyes. Also, the picture on the site looks like Simon. Granted, he's not as clean-shaven in the police photo in the file, but it's him," Kathy assured them as she dug out the contact information she had collected. "I wrote down the information for his parents, Darren and Haley Bradwell. They live in Pennsylvania, and apparently, he's been missing for several years." She handed the contact information over to Bailey who read every syllable on that piece of paper.

"Have you contacted them yet?"

"No. I thought it would be best to give it to you first."

"This is good," he said smiling. "I'll give them a call as soon as I get back from court."

"I thought the trial was tomorrow?" Kathy said a little puzzled.

"It does; however, this is almost as important as the trial itself. Jury selection."

"Oh, right," Kathy said nodding her head. "I knew that. I did," she said as Vicky let a smile slip out.

Bailey chucked, "You stay on the case and call me with any more updates. Have you got a witness list?" he said heading for the door.

"Yes, I've got four names as a start. Charlie's wife and daughter, the gas station attendant, and the goodwill employee," Bailey nodded in approval. "and I'll probably drop by the police station at some point."

"Sounds good. I'll probably be tied up in court most of the day. Vicky, I need you to go meet our client and make sure there are no problems.

"Right," Vicky said grabbing her purse.

"Come on, Kathy," Bailey said as he escorted her out and closed the door.

"Well, good luck with the selection."

"Thanks, and now, I leave you in the capable hands of Sally," he said walking past the reception desk and out the door,

"Anything wrong?" Sally asked as Kathy leaned against the desk.

"No, everything is just great. Except, that I have to be a witness for D. A. Phillips."

"Tough break."

"That is such an understatement. Hey, Sally, how important is jury selection?"

"Well, from everything I've heard from Bailey and Vicky, it could very easily make or break a case."

"I thought Bailey looked a little tense.'

"Apparently, it is a delicate balance," Sally said as Kathy gave her a sideways glance. "Or so Bailey says."

"Alright, well, I've got four people to talk to, and none of them are here."

"Well, I am perfectly happy behind the desk," Sally stated taking a seat.

"You sure?" Kathy teased as Sally shook her head.

"See ya," Sally said as Kathy started for the door.

"Just let me know if you're ever ready for round two," Kathy replied as she walked out of the office and headed for her car. The first name on her list was Claire Schofield. *Let's see what you have to say*, she thought as she pulled out of the parking lot.

32

Kathy pulled into the driveway of 1216 Fairfield Drive, home of Claire Schofield. Kathy observed the grey stone house with light blue shutters. She also noticed the three cars in the driveway. Kathy walked up the drive and rang the doorbell. A pretty blonde lady opened the door.

"Yes?" she huffed.

"Are you Ms. Claire Schofield?"

"Who wants to know?" she shot back.

"I'm Kathy Hamilton. I'm an investigator for Bailey Clark's office."

"Really? Well, I've already given a statement to the police."

"Yes, but I'm...Mr. Clark is representing the defendant, and we do our own separate investigation. Just a few questions, and I'll be on my way."

"Well," she sighed. "As long as you're not a reporter. Come on in," she said as Kathy walked past her and sat down in the living room. "Okay, let's have it," she said lighting a cigarette.

"Alright," Kathy replied digging out her notepad. "How long were you married to Charlie?"

"You mean Charles?" Claire corrected. "I guess it's been, six years."

"How did he end up on the street?" Kathy asked noticing the surroundings she was sitting in. The whole house seemed to be nicely furnished, although she didn't see any family photos.

Claire took a drag of her cigarette, "It really is a long story. My Charles, once upon a time, was a successful doctor. Surgeon to be exact, and one day, he was faced with a malpractice lawsuit and our happy, little family went up in smoke." *Tread carefully,* Kathy thought to herself.

"So, when did you discover that Charlie had left?"

"I'm not sure about the exact day. About a year after the suit, he just left one day and never came back." Kathy tried not to comment as she took her notes. "It really was my saving grace. I tried to be the supportive wife and all, but it just wasn't working anymore," she said as she flicked her cigarette in the ashtray. Kathy jotted down some more notes and tried to not let her emotions show.

"I understand you have a daughter, Alyssa." The smile on Claire's face vanished.

"What about her?"

"I'd like to speak with her if I could?"

Claire put out her cigarette and got up, "I think you're done." Kathy picked up her bag as Claire showed her to the door.

"Thank you for your time," Kathy said as Claire closed the door on her.

"Well, that went well," Kathy remarked as she saw a man hammering a for sale sign in the front yard. *Claire's selling the house,* Kathy thought, *why is she in such a hurry to leave?* Kathy shook her head as she stepped off the front porch. She started toward her car when she heard a noise.

"Excuse me," a voice said and tapped Kathy on the shoulder.

"What the..." Kathy gasped.

"Jumpy much?" a young girl said as Kathy turned around.

"It's a long story," Kathy said getting her breath back. "You wouldn't be Alyssa, would you?" The girl nodded her head yes. "Your mom said you weren't at home."

"Mom says whatever's convenient at the time. I heard you asking questions about Dad, so I waited outside until Mom kicked you out."

"Oh, I'm glad someone saw that coming." Kathy took a good look at Alyssa and realized something; she looked exactly like Charlie. Her face was eerily similar with the same brown hair and eyes of her father.

"So, what did you want to know?"

"How did your dad end up on the street?"

"Well, everyone blames the lawsuit, but really, I blame

mom. Don't buy that act for a minute. The only thing she misses about Dad is his money." *No love lost there,* Kathy thought to herself.

"Did your Dad have any enemies?"

"Not really. The lawsuit took everything from Dad."

"What exactly happened?"

"I don't know all the details, but Mom's got all of Dad's files locked up in a file cabinet in the house. All I know is that the name of the family that brought the lawsuit was Addison and it had something to do with a surgery that Dad did."

"Okay," Kathy said jotting down some notes.

"Miss Kathy?"

"Yeah, what is it?"

"There's one more thing," she said and pulled a note from her pocket. "Dad left me this." Kathy tried not to stare at the piece of paper.

"He left you a note. When?"

"I found it in the visor of my car Thursday morning."

"May I see it?"

"Only if you give it right back." Kathy nodded and Alyssa gently placed the note in Kathy's hand. Kathy carefully opened it and read what was probably Charlie's last words.

To my babygirl,

I know I have no right to speak to you but please hear me out. I only want to tell you two things. One: I'm sorry for leaving you. God help me, I am so sorry, I don't ask for your forgiveness because I don't forgive myself. Two: I love you No matter what your mother

tells you, I love you more than you know. Please remember me as I was before things went bad. The good times in the park, just me and you. I have to go now - I don't have any more time.
With all my heart,

Dad

P.S. If you meet a girl named Kathy tell her that the man who killed the girl in the alley didn't have red hair. It wasn't Chase.

A small tear slid down Kathy's cheek as she gently folded the note and handed it back to Alyssa

"Thank you."

"Are you going to find who killed my dad?" Alyssa asked quietly.

"I'm actually here to prove that our client is innocent of Charlie's murder but..."Kathy saw Alyssa's face drop. "I'm looking into it anyway." Alyssa raised her head and smiled.

"Thanks. I gotta go before Mom sees," she said and quickly disappeared behind the house.

Kathy got into her car and tried to compose herself. She felt terrible for Alyssa and couldn't imagine losing her own dad. Claire Schofield, however, was another matter. *That lady lied to me,* Kathy thought and started the engine. *She is hiding something, and I'm gonna find out what it is.*

33

It was rush hour lunchtime at Delany's when Kathy walked in. She had phoned Michael, and he had happily agreed to meet for lunch and drag his partner along. Kathy saw them both at the bar, so she helped herself.

"Hey guys," she said as Michael pulled out her chair.

"Hey, yourself. You don't look as bad as you sounded on the phone."

"That's my partner's try at a compliment," Jamie said with a smile.

"It's fine, I'm used to him by now. I've been interviewing witnesses, and it's been....interesting," she said as Sam came over.

"Hey, Kathy, what can I get ya?"

"Just a cheeseburger and Pepsi. Thanks. How have you been?"

"Better. I heard you've had a surprise of your own."

"Yes, and I'm not likely to forget it."

"Well as everyone keeps telling me, it just takes time. Be back in a few with your order," she said as she walked away.

"So, you're having witness trouble, huh?" Michael asked taking a sip of his drink.

"You could say that."

"Me and Jamie here are experts when it comes to witnesses."

"Really?" Kathy said grinning, waiting for the punchline

"Absolutely," Jamie chimed in. "See we have this routine, and it is guaranteed to work."

"Please do tell."

"See, there lies the rub. If we give away our secret, then our luck will run out and then we'll get fired and won't be able to pay our bills...so you know what that means."

"I'll probably regret it, but what?"

"Michael and I will have to move all our stuff to your apartment," Jamie said grinning.

"Oh no. You guys are full of it," Kathy said throwing a crumpled napkin at them. "However, somehow I don't think Stacey would be all that upset," she replied as they all laughed. The laughter was quickly interrupted by the sound of a police radio.

"Are you kidding me?" Kathy huffed.

"Sorry, Kathy. Our lunch break is practically over anyway," he said laying his money on the table. "Make sure it gets to the right person, okay."

"Michael looks like another domestic," Jamie said as he put the radio back on his belt.

"Yeah, copy that," Michael said putting on his jacket.

"And how much of this is my tip?" Kathy asked as Michael gave her a quick kiss and they hurried out the door. Kathy sighed as she watched them vanish out of sight.

"What happened to the guys?" Sam asked as she sat Kathy's burger and Pepsi down.

"That radio called, and they ran. Here's their bill money," she said handing it over to Sam. "How are things between you and Kevin?"

"Good. Really good."

"Well, that sounds promising."

"Kathy don't jinx me, but yeah he's been spending more time at my place. I just can't imagine my day without him anymore. It just goes to show you that if you wait for the right moment, anything can happen."

"I guess you're right," Kathy said taking a sip of her drink. "Hey, while you're here, does the name Claire Schofield ring a bell?"

"Claire Schofield? Not sure, what does she look like?"

"Blond hair, blue eyes, very expensive tastes, and she has a certain air about her." Sam puzzled over the description, went over to the cash register, and returned with a receipt.

"Here it is," she said holding the receipt. "She was in here last week. I sat them in a booth, and she definitely had a "certain air" that I didn't care for," Sam replied as Kathy stopped eating.

"Did you say them?"

"Ah, you caught that?"

"Spill it," Kathy said taking out her notepad.

"Claire Schofield was not dining alone. There was a rather good-looking guy with her, and before you ask, all I heard was she called him Mark."

"Mark, huh," Kathy said soaking up every word Sam said.

"Uh-huh, however, his full name is on the receipt. Mark Daniels."

"What did this Mark Daniels look like?"

"Blond hair, blue eyes, and definitely would turn heads if you know what I mean. He also didn't seem to be hurting for money."

"I gotcha ya," Kathy said nodding her head. "Well, Claire certainly forgot to tell me about this."

"Oh, gotta go. Let me know if you need anything else," Sam said as she went to take care of the customers at the other end of the bar.

Kathy finished her burger as Sam's words kept rolling around in her head. *The right moment*, Kathy thought, *is that what you did Claire Schofield? Did you just wait for the right moment?* Kathy wasn't sure, all she knew was that Claire was hiding something, and it was more than just a handsome fellow.

34

Bailey leaned back in his office chair and closed his eyes. He had been working for six straight hours, and he felt like his eyes were about to roll out of his eyes. He had gone several rounds with the D. A. over the jury selection and wanted to strangle the D. A.'s neck by the time it was over. His client, on the other hand, hadn't said a word. He just sat there and stared at the defense table. Bailey didn't know what to make of his new client. He sat back up and looked over the various papers scattered across his desk. *Somewhere in there is the answer to the case*, he thought and finally remembered the number Kathy had given him. He grabbed his legal pad and dialed the number for the Bradwell's. The phone rang several times and he hoped that this wouldn't turn out to be a dead-end.

"Hello?" a tired male voice finally answered.

"Hello. Is this the residence of Darren and Haley Bradwell?" Bailey asked hopefully.

"Listen if you're a reporter, please leave us alone. We can't take it anymore!"

"No, wait!" Bailey interrupted. "My name is Bailey Clark and I'm a lawyer. Do you have a son by the name of Simon?" There was a brief pause.

"Simon," the voice repeated. "Please, sir, don't play games. Did you really find our boy?"

"Yes, sir. I believe so. He is thirty-one years old, brown hair and eyes."

"Haley!" the voice yelled, "They've found him! They've finally found him!" Bailey heard some rustling noises before the voice came back. "You said your name was Bailey?"

"Yes, sir. Bailey Clark."

"Just tell us where you are, and we'll come to get our boy."

"I'm afraid, sir, it's not that simple, Bailey replied knowing the inevitable reaction.

"What do you mean?" he asked getting upset.

"First of all, I am a lawyer in North Carolina; and second, I am trying to defend Simon on a murder charge." The line went silent except for the sound of breathing. "Are you still there?"

"A murder charge," he finally said. "What do you mean, what has happened?"

"It's a long story for a phone conversation. However, if you and Mrs. Bradwell are able, I would like for you both to come to North Carolina and help me with your son's case."

"Mr. Clark, we have waited for years to hear anything about our son. We will be on the next flight out."

"Thank you, Mr. Bradwell. I will send you my office address, so come here first. Together, we will try to bring your son home."

35

The bell rang as Kathy walked into Freddie's Quickstop, she saw a young girl behind the counter and hoped she'd have better luck than with her first.

"Hi, are you Sophie Ramirez?" Kathy asked when she came to the counter.

"Uh-huh. You need something?"

"My name is Kathy Hamilton. I'm working with the lawyer, Bailey Clark, on a case and I was wondering if I could ask you a few questions."

"Sure. Hey, Tyler, cover for me," she called over her shoulder and a young guy came out.

"I have five more minutes on my break," he huffed.

"Stop it. I'll make it up to you. I swear," she reassured him as he begrudgingly took the register, and Sophie took Kathy to the back of the store. "So, what do you need to know?"

"Do you remember seeing this man here?" Kathy asked holding up a picture of Charlie. Sophie looked at the photo for a few minutes.

"Yeah, he's been here several times."

"Really. When was the last time?"

"Maybe about a week ago, but..."

"But what?"

"He wasn't in the store. I saw him at the payphone outside."

"How long was he there?" Kathy said taking notes.

"Maybe, fifteen minutes, I think."

"Did you see anybody with him?"

"I don't think so, but I wasn't paying attention the whole time." Kathy was a little disappointed but pulled out another picture for Sophie to look at.

"How about this guy?" Kathy asked holding up Simon's picture. The picture was a mugshot, but that was the only picture she had. Sophie's eyes widened when she saw the photo.

"This guy does seem familiar. Did he do something?"

"Not sure," Kathy replied. "What do you remember about him?"

"I've only seen him hovering around the dumpster outside. He never comes in the store, and I don't think he likes people very much."

"What makes you say that?" Kathy asked puzzled.

"Well, it's just every time someone would get close to

him, he'd duck or runoff," Kathy jotted down every word Sophie was saying.

"Last question, do you have any security cameras here?"

"Are you kidding?" Sophie said with a laugh. "Freddie wouldn't let us be open without one. He's had some trouble with people running off without paying at the pumps, and he's so tight-fisted that if one penny was missing, he'd know it. There's one directly behind the register, and the other one keeps an eye on the pumps." Kathy went to the window and looked out.

"Hey, Sophie, would the payphone be in view of the camera?" Kathy asked as Sophie came over to take a look.

"Umm, possibly. Let's go see," she said as she took Kathy into the backroom.

Sophie hit the play button on the security footage, and they both watched the screen intently as the footage began to roll. To Kathy's disappointment, only the bottom half of the payphone was visible. She continued to watch until she saw half a figure go into the payphone and stay there for about twelve minutes. Then suddenly, the same figure ran off and left the receiver dangling in the booth,

"That's weird," Sophie commented as Kathy stepped a little closer to the screen. The tape was a little fuzzy, but Kathy would swear that there were a pair of shoes that came into view then slowly disappeared.

"Hey, Sophie, is there any way I can get a copy of this?" Kathy asked putting away her notepad.

"I gotta ask Freddie," she said throwing up her hands.

"Please, I'll wait," Kathy answered as Sophie went to make the call. Kathy knew that somebody was after Charlie and here was possibly the first piece of evidence to prove it.

36

It was almost three o'clock when Kathy pulled into the parking lot of the local Goodwill store. It was appropriately located next to St. Mary's Cathedral, the only Catholic church in town. Kathy slung her bag on her shoulder and made her way inside. As she opened the door, she noticed a few customers milling around, and then saw the two women at the counter.

"Hi," Kathy said walked over. "Is there a Lynn Taylor here?" The two women looked at each other.

"I'm Lynn," the brunette said. "How can I help you?" she added with a smile.

"My name is Kathy Hamilton, and I'm working on a case for Bailey Clark. Could I ask you a few questions?" Lynn looked at her co-worker with pleading eyes.

"It'll take just a few minutes."

"Okay," she said as Lynn walked out from behind the counter and took Kathy to a quiet corner in the back of the store.

"How long have you worked here?"

Lynn smiled, "Probably, eight years now." Kathy dug out Charlie and Simon's photos from her bag.

"Have you seen either one of these two here at the store?" Lynn took the pictures and the smile on her face faded away.

"Yes. Both of them come around pretty regularly."

"Why?"

"They usually scavenger in the clothing barrels, especially in the winter. It just breaks your heart, doesn't it? I try to bring them some food when I can, but there's only so much you can do."

"Does anything stand out about either one?"

"Charlie was always friendly. I mean, he smelled of alcohol, but he would never hurt anybody."

"And the other one?"

"Simon is a different story." *Uh-oh*, Kathy thought as she continued her notetaking. "He doesn't talk to people except to me. Don't ask me why. He's always fidgeting, and he does not like crowds."

"So, you wouldn't call Simon friendly then?"

Lynn exhaled, "Just distant. He did get into a fight with Charlie once." *Not what I wanted to hear*, Kathy thought to herself. "It was November, and the wind was colder than usual. We had just put out some heavy coat donations, and there was a green one that both of them wanted. I thought I was going to have to call for help, but Simon finally pulled it away from Charlie."

"Anyone get hurt?" Kathy asked not sure she wanted to hear the answer.

"No," Lynn said shaking her head. "Then I saw Simon get rid of his old coat and put something into the pocket of his new one."

"What was it?"

"Couldn't really see, and I wasn't going to ask him at that moment."

"Do you remember seeing Simon here last Thursday from eight p.m. to midnight?"

"Umm, not sure," Lynn said looking at her watch. "I don't think so. I'm sorry, I really have to get back to the counter or my co-worker is going to get me in trouble."

"Well, thank you for your time, Ms. Taylor," Kathy said putting away her notepad.

"No problem. Have a good day," she said as she watched Kathy go out the door and out of sight. Lynn thought back to the fight between Charlie and Simon. She had never seen Simon so angry. Lynn honestly asked herself if Simon could've hurt Charlie, and it bothered her that she couldn't say without a doubt no.

37

Kathy finally walked through her apartment door at six-thirty in the evening, and the first thing she noticed was the smell of food in the air.

"Stace, are you here?" Kathy called out as she closed the door.

"Yep, and I have treats."

"Sounds fantastic," she replied as she tossed her bag on the couch and took a seat at the kitchen table. "So, what's on the menu?"

"We have buffalo wings in two flavors, spicy for those of us who like adventure and mild for those who prefer a safer option."

"Thanks for the subtle hint," Kathy said smiling.

"And last but certainly not least, cheese fries."

"You are the perfect roommate, aren't you," Kathy commented grabbing a plate.

"True, very true," Stacey replied and pulled the spicy wings closer. "So, did anything interesting happen today?"

"I had four interviews today, and I think one of them is hiding something."

"Really? Do tell," Stacey said fully intrigued.

"I was talking to Claire Schofield, Charlie's wife, this morning and I just got the feeling she was being less than honest."

"Why would you say that?" Stacey asked, wiping sauce off of her mouth.

"Because after Claire's story, I spoke with her daughter Alyssa and she basically called her mom a liar and an actress."

"So, I take it that they're not BFFs."

"Anything but," Kathy said scooping up some cheese fries onto her plate. "So, Claire says that the malpractice suit was causing their marriage problems, but according to Alyssa, the only thing Claire misses was Charlie's money."

"Interesting."

"Oh, and I stopped by Delany's for lunch, and Sam mentioned that a woman matching Claire's description has been coming in with another man, a Mark Daniels."

"Now this story is getting good," Stacey said with a gleam in her eye. "Who is this mystery man?"

"Don't worry; he is at the top of my list. Also, I may have found some interesting footage from Freddie's Quickstop, but I need to run it by Bailey first."

"Fine," Stacey said deflated. "I guess I understand."

"How about you? Any progress on the candidates?"

"Actually, yes. I've already interviewed my first candidate, Terrance Williams. His answers were really vague, and he is running a smear campaign against one of his competitors. He has a family, so I was hoping to get some quotes from them, but Mr. Williams said they were not available for comment, which makes me think there's something there he doesn't want me to see."

"I have no doubt that you will sniff it out," Kathy said eating her last buffalo wing.

"Trust me, I will. I'm going to take another shot at him tomorrow before I start writing the profile. Then, on to the next one," Stacey said with glee.

"Good grief. Anyway, I need to update Bailey on what I found today before it gets too late."

"Okay, I'll be in the living room watching unsolved crimes and devouring the rest of the cheese fries, if anybody is interested," she said peering over at Kathy.

"You better not eat all those fries," Kathy warned her. "I will be back; you just save me a seat and some cheese fries," she called out as she picked up her bag and headed for her bedroom. She dialed Bailey's number hoping it wouldn't go to voicemail. It rang several times before his voice came over the line.

"Hello?"

"Hi, Bailey, it's Kathy. Just thought I would let you know what happened today."

"Okay, what have you got?" Kathy thought he sounded a bit tired.

"I spoke to all of the witnesses on my list. Claire Schofield is a piece of work. She claims that the malpractice suit against Charlie is what caused their marriage problems, but the daughter says that her mom is lying and when I went to Delany's for lunch, Sam told me that Claire has been there with a guy named Mark Daniels."

"Interesting. Mark Daniels, you say."

"Now, I don't have proof yet, but it seems to me like Claire is hiding something, and not just Mark Daniels."

"Okay, anything else?"

"I have some footage of someone at the payphone at Freddie's Quickstop at the same time that Charlie is supposed to be there; however, you can't see their face. The Goodwill employee, Lynn, said that she didn't remember Simon there at the time of the murder, but she didn't sound too sure."

"Nice job, Miss Kathy. Vicky and I will follow up with this. See if you can nail down where our client was at the time of the murder and take another shot at the Goodwill employee."

"Alright, consider it done."

"Thanks for the work. Have a good night, Miss Kathy," he said he hung up.

Kathy put away her cell phone and quickly decided to get back to the living room before all the cheese fries were gone. Bailey had sounded so worn out, she hoped the information she gave him would help.

Thursday, April 24th

38

It was exactly seven o'clock when Kathy woke up to the sound of her alarm clock. As she looked at the alarm on her cell, she noticed a calendar notification had popped up, it read:

Be @ courthouse 9 am

"Oh, no," she groaned. "It's today." She begrudgingly rolled out of bed and turned off the alarm. As she quickly got dressed, she noticed that her hand started to sweat. "Don't do this, Kathy," she said out loud. "Just focus."

Kathy found Stacey at the kitchen table with a muffin and cup of coffee in hand. "Okay, I need help," she said as Stacey looked up.

"Of course, you do, with what?"

"Be serious," Kathy said sternly. "I have to go to court today, and I need you to tell me if I look like a credible witness."

Stacey paused for a few minutes as she looked at the black dress pants and dark purple dress shirt Kathy had picked out. "Well?" Kathy asked impatiently. "Do I look believable, credible?"

"Definitely certifiable," Stacey said with a grin.

"Stacey!"

"Alright, alright. Absolutely, one hundred percent credible," Stacey said seriously.

"Thanks," Kathy replied taking a deep breath.

"You going to make it?"

"Yes. Yes, I am. All I have to do is remember the Bailey and Vicky approved responses and it will all be fine."

"Yeah, okay," her roommate said as she got up from the table and went to the fridge.

"What are you doing?"

"Getting you some backup," Stacey replied as she tossed her a Pepsi from the fridge. "You might need it."

"Right, thanks," Kathy said acknowledging the point. "Okay, I'll call you when it's over."

"Good luck. See ya."

"Thanks," Kathy said as she made her way to the door. *Okay, Kathy, don't screw this up. Just remember what Vicky said. Don't screw this up*, she thought to herself, as she closed the door behind her.

39

Kathy stepped off the courthouse elevator and made her way to Courtroom C. When she saw Bailey and Vicky in the hallway, she smiled.

"Morning," Bailey said when he saw Kathy walking toward them.

"Morning."

"So, the word is that you are second on the witness list for today."

"Great. Who has the pleasure of being first?"

"Detective McMannis," Bailey replied looking at his watch.

"Oh, this day keeps getting better and better."

"Just remember," Vicky chimed in. "Only answer the question, don't volunteer information, and breathe," she said with a reassuring smile.

"I got it. Thanks," Kathy replied with a nod.

"Well, ladies, shall we proceed? Judge Allan won't like it if we're not on time," Bailey said as he straighten his tie. Kathy started to feel a little better when someone caught her eye, D.A. Phillips in a pin-striped suit. As he got closer, he nodded to Kathy and stopped directly in front of Bailey.

"Well, Mr. Clark. Shall we do battle?" he asked with a smirk and disappeared into the courtroom, his A.D.A following close behind. *Jesus help me*, Kathy thought to herself, as she stared at the swinging courtroom door.

40

"All rise. The Court of the Fourth Judicial Circuit, Criminal Division, is now in session, the Honorable Walter Allan presiding," the bailiff called out as everyone stood up in unison. Kathy was two rows behind the defense table and peered around the man seated in front of her when the judge came out. Judge Allan looked to be in his mid-fifties and, from what Bailey said, he ran a tight courtroom

"Be seated," Judge Allan said as he sat down himself. "Mr. Parker, what is today's case?"

"Your Honor, today's case is The State of North Carolina versus Simon Bradwell."

"Very well. Ah, good morning Mr. Phillips. Is the state ready?"

"Yes, Your Honor," the D.A. said with a nod.

"Mr. Clark, is the defense ready?"

"Yes, Your Honor," Bailey said flatly.

"Very well. We will proceed to opening statements, Mr. Phillips," the judge declared as the D. A. got up and confidently walked in front of the jury box.

"Ladies and Gentleman of the jury, the State intends to prove to you, beyond a shadow of a doubt, that the defendant, Simon Bradwell, is guilty of first-degree murder. The State will provide witnesses and irrefutable facts that will lead every single one of you to the same conclusion. Now, I implore you not to be persuaded by the tactics the defense will use to shift your focus from things that they don't want you to see. Instead, look at the evidence and if you do that, there will be justice. Justice for Charlies Goldson and justice for his family. Thank you." As D.A. Phillips finished, Kathy looked at the jury and noticed that every one of them was intently listening to every word he said. *Oh, Bailey*, Kathy thought, *please be good.*

"Mr. Clark," the judge said, "you may proceed." Bailey got up and instead of walking toward the jury box, he stood behind his client.

"Ladies and Gentlemen of the jury, there are only two words I want you to remember: circumstantial and convenient." Bailey put his hands on Simon's shoulders and continued, "My client is here because he was a convenient target, and not because he has done anything wrong." Bailey then slowly made his way to the jury box, maintaining his eye contact with the jury. "And this irrefutable evidence the State has alluded to, we, the defense, will prove that it is not fact, but circumstantial evidence that could be used to prove anyone guilty of this horrible crime. Should someone pay for the murder of Charles Goldson? Absolutely, but not my client." Bailey scanned the jurors in the box, "No, the real murderer of Charles Goldson should be on trial for this crime. Ladies and Gentlemen, I ask you to really listen to what the State has to say and remember these two words: circumstantial and convenient. Thank you."

As Bailey went back to the defense table, Kathy let a smile slip onto her face. She had never heard Bailey in action, but if his opening statement was this good, then Simon might just have a real chance.

"The prosecution may call your first witness," Judge Allan said as D.A. Phillips stood up.

"Thank you, Your Honor. The State calls Detective McMannis to the stand." Kathy turned around as she heard the detective walk up, but he didn't look like Detective McMannis. This guy was wearing a pressed blue suit with his detective's badge hung in the pocket. *Talk about night and day*, Kathy thought, as the detective stepped into the witness box and was sworn in by the bailiff. D. A. Phillips and McMannis nodded to each other as the D. A. began his examination.

"Would you please state your name for the record?"

"William McMannis. I am a detective with the Rosemont Police Department."

"How many years have you worked in law enforcement?"

"Over ten years," he said proudly.

"You must have seen quite a few homicides in those ten years?"

"Yes, sir. I've lost count," McMannis answered as D. A. Phillips went over to the prosecution table and picked up a plastic bag.

"Do you recognize this, detective?"

"Yes, sir. That is the murder weapon we found at the crime scene."

"Could you describe the weapon for the jury?"

"It's called a shiv. A metal blade that has duct tape wrapped around it to form a handle. They are generally used in jails, prison, or by degenerates."

Bailey flew out of his chair, "Objection, Your Honor. Where are we going with this line of questioning?"

"Sustained," Judge Allan said as he looked at the D.A. "Let's move on."

"Where was the shiv found?"

"It was found at the scene in the possession of the defendant."

"Were there fingerprints found on the murder weapon?"

"Yes, sir. We found fingerprints matching the defendant."

"Would you consider a shiv to be an effective weapon?"

Bailey stood up, "Objection, Your Honor. Detective McMannis is hardly a weapons expert."

"Your Honor," D.A. Philips interrupted, "Detective McMannis is an experienced and respected member of the police who has seen countless weapons of all descriptions."

"Overruled," the judge declared as Bailey sat back down a little irritated.

"Now, detective, would you consider this to be an effective weapon?"

"Yes, sir. It may be homemade, but don't let that fool you for a second. It is very effective."

"You said that you found the murder weapon in the possession of the defendant."

"Yes, sir."

"So, where did you find the defendant?"

"When we got to the crime scene, we were sweeping the area and that's when one of the officers found the defendant, Simon Bradwell, behind the abandoned building holding the knife."

"Did you arrest him at this point?"

"Yes, sir. Two officers finally took him into custody while I collected the shiv as evidence."

"You said 'finally'. Can you explain for the jury?"

"The defendant was shoving, shouting, and trying to escape."

"What was the defendant shouting?"

McMannis paused and turned to look at the jury, "He said 'it's mine, give it back.'" D. A. Phillips walked over to the jury box and placed both hands on the bar.

"'It's mine, give it back.' Thank you, detective," D.A. Phillips said as he sat down with a look of pure confidence.

"Mr. Clark, you may cross," Judge Allan said as Bailey

buttoned his jacket.

"Detective McMannis, did you run a background check on my client, Simon Bradwell?"

"Yes, it is standard procedure."

"And what did you find?"

"Except for two speeding tickets, nothing."

"Really," Bailey said with exaggeration. "Not even a previous misdemeanor?"

"No."

"Interesting. So, my client went from not having a criminal history to being charged for first-degree murder. Now, detective, were there shoeprints found at the crime scene?" Detective McMannis shifted in his chair.

"Yes."

"What kind?"

"We found shoeprints that matched the victim, the defendant, and there was one set of prints that we couldn't match to anyone."

"Really. Why not?"

"That last set was a little larger than the defendant, but there were a lot of people in that area, and it was a dirt floor."

"I see. Did you find any blood spatter on my client's clothes when you took him into custody?"

"No," McMannis said with a scowl on his face.

"You didn't find a drop anywhere?"

"As I said, no, we did not."

"How do you explain that detective?"

"Maybe, he overpowered the victim or was wearing a covering that he discarded before we got there. I'm not sure," McMannis stated as Bailey went to the defense table.

"Detective, could you tell the jury what this is?"

"It's a piece of a plastic tie."

"And where was it found?"

"It was found at the crime scene next to the column where the victim was found," McMannis said sternly.

"Is it possible that a plastic tie was used on the victim as a restraint?"

"Yes, it's possible."

"How would my client have purchased these ties?"

"I'm not sure. Maybe, he found some in a dumpster somewhere," the detective replied getting agitated.

"One last question, detective. Is it reasonable to think that my client could have used something like this?"

"He has two hands. Anybody with two hands could do it."

"Yes, anybody could have done it. So, maybe there was somebody else there. You just picked the convenient one," Bailey stated as D.A. Phillips jumped out of his chair.

"Objection!"

"I have no more questions, Your Honor," Bailey said as he went back to the defense table.

"You may step down, detective," Judge Allan said as McMannis stepped out of the witness box. McMannis glared at Bailey as he passed by and re-took his seat in the gallery.

Judge Allan glanced at his watch, "I know it's a bit early, but we'll take a break for lunch. Court will resume at one o'clock sharp," he said as he struck the gavel. Kathy took a deep breath as people started to move around. She slowly found her way to Bailey and Vicky.

"Wow," she said as Bailey smiled. "That was impressive."

"Thank you. Let's hope the jury thought so too. Now, let's go get some lunch," he said as they all filed out of the courtroom.

41

Winchester had just walked back into his motel room when his cell started ringing. He looked at the number and recognized it immediately.

"Yes, boss."

"Are things on schedule?"

"Yes, boss."

"Well done, Winchester. Now, I have another situation that needs your attention. I will call again with the details, so be ready to move."

"I'll be waiting," he replied as the line went dead. Winchester opened up the sub he had gotten and grabbed a beer from the mini-fridge. As he casually ate his long-overdue meal, he took out his kit and carefully cleaned it. As he saw the light reflect off the knife blade, he smiled. He recalled how that homeless troublemaker had struggled as he slowly slid the blade across his throat. Winchester had wanted to use his own blade, but it wouldn't have fit the story he was trying to tell. The shiv was the perfect weapon, so convenient and will direct the cops far away from him. He chuckled to himself, reveling in the beauty of his plan. He sometimes wished that they would figure it out, just so he would have the challenge, but he knew better. The first lesson his handler had taught him was the best jobs are when no one knows you were even there. Remember that, don't get caught up in the moment. Use your head, and you will go far. He could still hear his handler's voice in his head, and he had come very far from where he started.

Winchester tossed the empty sub wrapper away and decided to take a quick nap. He had some time before his next assignment. He hoped it would be a good one.

42

"All rise. Court is now in session, the Honorable Walter Allan presiding," the bailiff called out as everyone stood up in unison.

"Be seated," Judge Allan said as he took his seat on the bench. "D.A. Phillips are you ready to proceed?"

"Yes, Your Honor."

"Then, call your next witness."

"The State calls Kathy Hamilton to the stand." Kathy took a deep breath and slowly got to her feet. She made her way to the witness box and stopped as the bailiff swore her to tell the truth. Kathy took her seat and tried to remember everything Vicky had told her. *Just remember*, she thought, *just answer the question, and breathe*. Kathy looked straight ahead as the D.A. approached her.

"Would you please state your name for the record?"

"Kathy Hamilton."

"Where do you work, Miss Hamilton?"

Kathy's eyes glanced over at the defense table, "I work as an investigator for Bailey Clark."

"Uh-huh, and do you know the deceased, Charles Goldson?" he asked walking in front of her view of the defense table.

"Well, I knew him as Charlie, but yes I know of Charles Goldson."

"Know of him, you say," the D. A. grinned. "How do you know of him?"

"I was trying to locate him in connection with another case as a witness," Kathy replied hoping she wasn't saying too much.

"Did you ever have any contact with the deceased?" *Oh boy*, Kathy thought, *here we go.*

"I talked with him twice on the phone in an effort to arrange a meeting."

"So, did you or did you not meet with the deceased?"

"We had finally arranged a time, but it was too late," Kathy replied trying to keep her voice even.

"Too late? What do you mean?"

"When I got there, he was dead."

"Can you recall, for the jury, what you saw?" D. A. Phillips said as he turned away from Kathy and focused on the jury.

"Objection, Your Honor!" Bailey stood up, "This testimony is highly prejudicial and graphic. The medical examiner can relate any necessary information regarding the manner of Mr. Goldson's death."

"Your Honor," the D.A. said as he whirled back around, "the description of this vicious crime is essential to the state's case."

"Overruled," the judge stated. D.A. Phillips nodded his head in relief and turned back to the jury.

"Miss Hamilton, what did you see?"

"I went to the abandoned strip mall to meet Charlie; I mean, Charles Goldson. I walked in and called out his name, but I didn't hear anything. I kept walking until...," her voice trailed off.

"Until what, Miss Hamilton?"

"I saw him leaned up against a concrete column. There was blood everywhere. He had been cut by the throat and in the stomach, it seemed," Kathy said as she wiped a small tear from her cheek.

"What day was this?"

"Umm, it was Friday. Friday, April the 18th."

"Did you see anybody else at the crime scene?" D.A. Phillips asked looking at the defendant.

"Umm, no."

"Uh-huh. Did you see anything unusual next to the victim's body?"

"There was a message written in the dirt."

"Your Honor," D. A. Phillips said taking a photo from the A.D.A, "the state would like to enter this photo as state's Exhibit C."

"So entered," the judge said as D.A. Phillips approached Kathy.

"Miss Hamilton, can you read what was written for the jury?" Kathy looked at the photo, but she didn't have to. Those words were still burned into her memory.

"It said, 'I saw him.'"

"I saw him. Do you have any idea as to what he meant?"

"Umm, I'm not sure," Kathy replied glancing over at Bailey.

"Objection, Your Honor," Bailey said standing up. "Calls for speculation. Miss Hamilton can't possibly know what the victim intended to say."

"Sustained," the judge said, "Move on Mr. Phillips."

"That's okay, Your Honor. I have one final question. Miss Hamilton, when you discovered the body of Mr. Goldson, did you see anything that would suggest a third person had been there?" D. A. Phillips asked with a grin. Kathy hated the answer she was about to give. *Hateful man*, she thought; she had found the plastic tie when she came back to the crime scene.

"No."

"I see. No evidence of a third person. Maybe that's because there isn't one. I have no more questions for this witness, Your Honor," D. A. Phillips stated as he took his seat at the prosecution table.

"Your witness, Mr. Clark," Judge Allan said as Bailey stood up.

"Thank you, Your Honor," Bailey replied as he shot the D.A. a hard look. Miss Hamilton, how long have you tried to find Mr. Goldson?"

"About two weeks."

"How many times did you have contact with him?"

"Two actual phone conversations and one voicemail he left on my cell."

"Were these long or short conversations?"

"Objection, Your Honor," the D.A. said as he stood up. "What is the relevance?"

"Mr. Clark," Judge Allan said, "I presume this line of questioning is going somewhere."

"Absolutely, Your Honor. Very quickly."

"Proceed," the judge sighed.

"Miss Hamilton, were they long or short conversations?"

"They were short. He even hung up on me once."

"Why were they so short?"

"He said someone was after him."

"Really," Bailey said looking at the D.A. "Did he say who was after him?"

"No, but he said that somebody was chasing him."

"Interesting," Bailey said with a smile. "Now, Miss Hamilton, you have been helping with the investigation for the defense, is that not correct?"

"Yes," Kathy said smiling. She much preferred to be

questioned by Bailey any day.

"Did you interview any witnesses regarding the defendant, Mr. Bradwell?"

"I did."

"How did they describe him?"

"They described him as a loner, that he kept to himself, and he didn't like to be around a lot of people."

"Did they describe him as a violent person?" Bailey asked turning his attention to the jury.

"No, sir."

"Did they describe him as a confrontational person?"

"No, sir. They never said anything like that."

"Thank you, Miss Hamilton. It makes one wonder how a non-violent person could commit such a violent crime. I have no further questions," Bailey said as Kathy was excused from the witness stand. As Kathy passed Bailey at the defense table, he gave her a quick wink. Kathy exhaled and took her seat in the gallery. *Glad that's over with*, she thought, as she heard the judge speak.

"Mr. Phillips, call your next witness."

"The state calls Claire Schofield to the stand." *This should be good*, Kathy thought, as Claire walked past her and took her seat in the witness box. Claire was in a nice dark blue pantsuit with minimal makeup. D.A. Phillips slowly approached the witness box.

"Can you please state your name for the record?"

"Claire Schofield?"

"What is your relationship to the deceased?"

"He was my husband."

"How long were you married?"

"We were married for about ten years," Claire replied demurely.

"Would you describe your marriage as a happy marriage?"

"At the beginning it was, but after the lawsuit, it just became too much. Charles was a respected doctor until a malpractice suit was filed against him. Charles was never the same after that."

"I can only imagine the toll that took on your family," D. A. Phillips said handing her a tissue.

"It was difficult," she said taking the tissue, "his drinking and depression just became too much." *Oh, good grief,* Kathy thought, *she should get an Oscar for this performance.*

"How long has it been since you have communicated with your husband?"

"It's been about five years."

"I guess it was quite a shock when the police told you that your husband was dead?"

"Yes, I could hardly believe what I was hearing."

"You have a daughter, is that right?"

"Yes, our Alyssa," she replied with a smile.

"Was your daughter close to her father?"

"Oh yes," Claire said with a sigh. "They were always together."

"So, it's safe to say that your family has seen quite a bit of tragedy."

"Objection!" Bailey said shooting out of his chair.

"I have no further questions, Your Honor.," D. A. Phillips said as he smiled on his way back to the prosecution table.

"Your witness, Mr. Clark," the judge said as Bailey stood up and made his way to the witness box.

"Ms. Schofield, you described your marriage as a happy one?"

"Objection," the D. A. called out, "already asked and answered."

"Your Honor, the D. A. opened the door, and this goes directly toward the credibility of the witness." Judge Allan paused for a moment.

"He has a point, Mr. Phillips. Continue, Mr. Clark."

"Thank you, Your Honor. Ms. Schofield, was your marriage a happy one?"

"It was until Charles started drinking," Claire retorted.

"Do you know a man named, Mark Daniels?"

"Yes," Claire said shifting in her seat.

"What is the nature of your relationship? Is it business or personal?"

"I...." Claire began to stammer.

"Isn't it true that you have been seeing this person for quite some time? Your Honor, I submit these telephone records into evidence as defense Exhibit B."

"So entered."

"Now, Ms. Schofield, would you describe your

relationship to Mr. Daniels as a personal one?"

"No."

"I see multiple calls listed here between you and Mr. Daniels. Calls that lasted hours. When did you first start seeing Mr. Daniels?"

Claire sighed, "Almost six years." Kathy heard a small gasp from the courtroom gallery.

"Order!" Judge Allan said striking the gavel. Kathy glanced at the jury; they were not happy.

"Six years," Bailey repeated. "So, maybe it was the affair and not the malpractice suit that caused the marriage problems." Claire just stared at Bailey. "Did you ever look for your husband?" Claire gave Bailey a hard look.

"Of course, we did. My daughter was heartbroken."

"I'm sure she was," Bailey replied. "Last question, Ms. Schofield, since you were less than forthcoming about your relationship with Mr. Daniels, what else are you not telling us?'

"Objection!" D. A. Phillips called out.

"Maybe, it also why you refer to yourself as Ms. Schofield and not Mrs. Goldson?"

"Your Honor!" D. A. Phillips said.

"I withdraw the question. No further questions, Your Honor," Bailey said as he sat back down at the defense table. Judge Allan excused Claire from the witness stand, and Kathy wished she knew what the jury was thinking.

"Well, I think that's enough for today," Judge Allan said looking at the clock. "Due to the lateness of the hour, court will resume tomorrow at nine a.m. Court is adjourned," he said as he struck the gavel. Kathy got up and slowly made her way to the defense table as the police led Simon away.

"So, how do you think it went?" Kathy asked as Bailey turned toward her.

"Not too bad. It's only day one. There's plenty of work left to do." Vicky came over and patted Kathy's shoulder.

"You did fine," she said with a smile.

"I sure hope so."

"Don't worry," Bailey interrupted. "Go home and get some rest. Tomorrow you need to solidify Simon's whereabouts."

"Okay, got it."

"There's still a card or two left to play. As someone once said, I have only begun to fight," Bailey stated as he grabbed his briefcase and headed out of the courtroom, Vicky trailing close behind. Kathy sure hoped he was right. The way D. A. Phillips was playing, that card Bailey was talking about better be an ace. Kathy feared that nothing less would do.

43

Bailey walked into his office and shut the door. He flopped into his desk chair and leaned his head back. The first day of court was always the worst because you never knew what antics the prosecution would pull. He pulled out the bottle of scotch from the bottom drawer and poured himself a small drink. "I must be a glutton for punishment," he said as he downed the drink.

He and Vicky had both pulled long hours trying to pull together a defense for this guy. "Why can't I have clients with rock-solid alibis?" he muttered as he put the scotch back in the drawer. Bailey shook his head as he pulled out his notes for tomorrow. He still had a lot of work to do to prove to this jury that Simon was innocent. Although, discrediting the former Mrs. Goldson did win some points and was the best part of his day.

Poor Charlie, he thought to himself, *his whole life was taken from him, and his wife could have cared less.* He had to win this case not just for Simon, but for Charlie as well. He knew all too well how a woman could take advantage and not give a damn, yep; he knew all too well.

44

Kathy started for her apartment, but halfway there she decided that she needed to see someone. She took out her cell and in five minutes, made dinner plans with her dad. When Kathy pulled into the driveway, she took a deep breath. There was something about being at home...it just felt right. She walked through the front door and smelled the pasta sauce coming from the kitchen.

"I'm here," she called out.

"Hey, honey. I'm in here," her dad's voice came from the kitchen. Kathy walked inside and found a bowl of mixed salad on the table and her dad standing over two pots on the stove.

"Wow, someone's been busy," she said smiling.

"Best I could do on short notice."

"Yeah, sorry about that."

"Don't be sorry. It's always nice to have you here."

"What can I do to help?" she said hanging her bag on a chair.

"Strain the pasta, and I'll get the sauce poured up." They both took a bowl of pasta and sat down at the table. "Not that I'm complaining, but what brought this visit about?"

"Busy day," she said sprinkling some cheese on her pasta. "I had to testify in court today."

"Oh, I see. What happened?"

"Bailey said I did fine. I just wish I could've had the evidence to blow that D.A. out of the courtroom."

"I take it that he's not your favorite," he remarked taking a bite of the penne pasta in front of him.

"No, he's not. If I never saw him again, it would be fine with me." Her dad grinned. "Speaking of seeing people, Michael said you came to the PD." Dr. Hamilton paused for a second, what was he going to say.

"Umm, I did drop in for a moment or two. I decided to hand over your mom's files."

"Really?"

"It was time to stop holding on to them."

"Dad is there...has there been anything new in mom's case?" she said hopefully. Dr. Hamilton took a breath and gently took his daughter's hand.

"No, I'm sorry Kathleen. There's nothing."

"Will we ever find out what happened?"

"Who knows? Now, I'm going to get more pasta. How

about you?" he said as he went to the stove to refill his bowl.

As the conversation shifted away from her mom's case and on to less dramatic topics, Kathy couldn't shake the feeling that something was off. She couldn't remember the last time her dad had called her Kathleen. As Kathy helped him clean up the kitchen, she couldn't get that conversation out of her head. She couldn't remember the last time her dad didn't tell her what was going on. *Forget it*, she thought, *you're getting paranoid. If there was something going on, Dad would tell me. He would never keep secrets.*

Friday, April 25th

45

There was no sunshine filtering in Kathy's bedroom when she woke up the next morning. She fumbled for her cell phone and turned off the alarm. As she looked at her phone, she noticed the date, the twenty-fifth of April. Kathy got dressed and put on her necklace. She traced the locket with her fingers and sighed, "I love you, Mama." Kathy still remembered the day her mom gave it to her; it was and would always be her favorite. She pushed away the memories for now and headed to the kitchen for breakfast.

She expected to find Stacey at her computer but found a sticky note on the kitchen table instead.

Hey Kathy-

Gone to do interviews. I'll call about dinner.

-Stace

Kathy poured herself a cup of coffee and picked up her bag. She didn't feel like eating, and she had to make one stop before she went to the office. This was one appointment that Kathy never missed.

46

Kathy picked up some tulips and lilies at the local flower market. She got out of the car and walked across the grass. She didn't come as much as she used to. Kathy felt guilty for not visiting, and when she did, the wound was reopened; it really was a no-win situation. She stopped in front of her mother's resting place and looked at the inscription on the tombstone. Colleen Hamilton, beloved wife, and mother. Kathy gently placed the flowers up against the tombstone and stepped back. "Happy birthday, Mama," she whispered. "I got you your favorite flowers." Two tears slowly ran down her cheek. "Oh, Mama, I miss you so much. It still hurts. I thought maybe when enough time had passed it would get a little better, but it still hurts. I wish I could see you again. There are so many things I wish I could've shared with you. Anyway, I'll always make sure you have flowers.

Something for pretty, just like you Mama. There's so much I want to say, but I can't. It's just too much. I love you, Mama. I gotta go; there's someone else I need to find." Kathy kissed her hand and placed it on the stone. The hardest part was always walking away, but she finally and regrettably turned away.

Kathy looked among the tombstone until she found what she was looking for. "Hey, Charlie," Kathy said stopping in front of a newly placed stone. "I don't really like this place, too many memories. Anyway, I'm sorry I couldn't help you, but I will find out who killed you. Your daughter will have answers." Kathy walked away, from yet another grave and headed for her car. As she got closer to her mom's grave, she saw someone else there standing in front of the tombstone. She looked closer and realized that it was her dad; they apparently had the same idea. She stopped walking and watched as he placed flowers next to hers. Kathy could tell that he was talking to her, but Kathy couldn't hear what he was saying. She decided not to intrude, slowly backed up, and took the long way around to her car. Apparently, time hadn't healed anything for him either.

47

It was still cloudy when Kathy walked into her office. Sally had told her that Bailey would be in court all day and Kathy knew she had plenty of work to do. She walked down the hallway, stepped inside her office, and immediately got to work. She took her notes out of her bag and went to her case board. "Okay," she said looking at her board. "Where was Simon? Sophie said she saw him at the Quickstop at eight o'clock, and the time of death for Charlie was..." she went back to her notes, "between eight p.m and twelve a.m." Kathy wrote the times on her case board, "That still leaves quite a few hours unaccounted for." Kathy looked at the photo of the murder weapon taped onto her case board. "Why would Simon be holding the murder weapon at the crime scene? Detective McMannis said that he was trying to clean it. None of that makes sense. Why would Simon stay at the crime scene if he did kill Charlie? Wouldn't he run away?" Kathy sat down at the desk and went back through her interview notes. "Wouldn't Simon have gone somewhere he felt safe?" Kathy stopped when she came across her notes on Lynn. "Lynn said she gave food to Simon, so Simon probably trusted her." Kathy looked through her notes and realized that Lynn never told her when she saw Simon. Kathy threw her notes in her bag and dashed out the door. She was going to find out if there was more to Lynn's story.

48

Lynn was going through a box of donations when she heard someone walk through the door. When she looked up and saw Kathy walking toward her, all of a sudden the room felt dramatically smaller.

"Hi, Kathy," she said trying to smile. "Is there something else I can help you with?"

"Actually, yes. I was wondering if you're remembered anything else about Simon?"

"Oh, umm..."

"You see there are just a few details about this case that are not adding up," Kathy said as Lynn fumbled with the shirt in her hands.

"I'm pretty sure...I..."

"Please," Kathy interrupted. "Lynn, if you know anything

else about the last time you saw Simon, please tell me. I just want to help him, I promise." Lynn looked at Kathy and couldn't take it anymore; if she lost her job, then so be it.

"Okay," she said taking a breath. "There are some things that I left out when I told you about Simon and Charlie being at the store. I left out the fact about why they were arguing."

"Okay, why?"

"I didn't hear all of it. All I know is that Simon kept accusing Charlie of taking something of his. He kept screaming you took it. I know you took it."

"Really," Kathy said getting more interested by the second. "Simon didn't say what it was?"

"No, but he was very upset about it. Charlie finally left; I stayed and tried to calm him down. It wasn't easy." she said hesitating.

"Lynn, I promise I only want to help Simon."

"I went in the breakroom and got him a sandwich and some hot chocolate. I thought maybe some food would take his mind off of whatever it was he lost."

"Do you bring him food often?"

"Sometimes, but please don't tell my boss. He doesn't like it when people like Simon camp out at the store."

"Lynn, did Simon stay at the store that night?" Kathy asked hopefully.

"Well, when I gave Simon the sandwich it was almost nine a.m. That's another reason why I did it. I usually close up, so no one sees it, but me. When I left for the night, I saw Simon behind the store settling down to sleep and when I came back the next morning, he was gone." Kathy took out her notepad and jotted down everything Lynn had just told her.

"Hey, Lynn, how long do you think it would take for someone like Simon to go from here to the abandoned mall?"

Lynn thought for a second, "Maybe about an hour, something like that."

"Uh-huh," Kathy said and she continued writing in her notepad. "Lynn, I'm going to tell Simon's lawyer, the one I work for, about this. If he called you, would you talk to him?" Lynn started fidgeting with her fingers.

"I just don't want to get into trouble. I really like my job." Kathy walked over and took her hands.

"I'm sure Bailey can work something out. We have to help Simon."

Lynn nodded, "You're right. Go ahead, I'll talk to him."

"Thank you, Lynn," Kathy exclaimed and gave her a hug. "Don't worry, everything will turn out alright." Kathy put up her notepad and looked at her watch, she was due back at the office. "I have to run, but I will let Bailey know, and thanks again," Kathy said running out the door.

Lynn watched her leave and sighed. She knew she was doing the right thing; she only hoped it wasn't too late.

49

It was after one o'clock in the afternoon before Kathy made it back to the office. For such a small town, Rosemont still had its moments of bad traffic. As she walked through the door, she saw Sally at the desk waving her over.

"Bailey's in his office. He has some visitors he wants you to meet," she said smiling.

"Sally, what's going on?"

"Not saying a word. That's part of my charm, I know when not to talk," she said with a wink. Kathy rolled her eyes.

"Yeah, okay Sally," she said walking back to Bailey's office. She knocked on the door and opened it when she heard Bailey's voice. She walked in and saw Bailey behind his desk, but there was also a couple sitting in the leather chairs across from him.

"Come on in, Kathy. I have some people I would like for

you to meet." Kathy closed the door and Bailey pulled up a third chair for her. "Kathy, I would like for you to meet Mr. and Mrs. Bradwell, Simon's parents." Kathy was glad she had already sat down because she felt her legs give under her. "This is Darren and Haley Bradwell. After you gave me the information you found on the missing persons website, I called, and here we are."

"She's the one?" Mrs. Bradwell said tearfully.

"Yes, ma'am. I was just doing my..." Kathy was cut off as Mrs. Bradwell gave Kathy the biggest hug she had ever had.

"Thank you so much. You have no idea how hard it has been not knowing what had happened to my boy. Thank you," she said as tears began to fall down her face. Kathy started to get emotional; she knew all too well what it was like not having answers.

"I'm just glad that I could help," she said as Mrs. Bradwell sat back down.

"Mr. Clark," Mr. Bradwell interrupted, "Where do we go from here?"

"That is an excellent question. That's why I asked you to come to my office. I wanted to ask Mrs. Bradwell if she would be able to testify in defense of her son." Mr. and Mrs. Bradwell glanced at each other.

"Do you think it would help?" Mr. Bradwell asked holding his wife's hand.

"I do. I need the jury to see who Simon really is, and there's nobody more able to do that than you, Mrs. Bradwell."

"If you think it will bring my boy home, I will do

whatever it takes," she replied.

"Good," Bailey said with a smile. "So, the plan is for you to testify, and I also got in touch with Simon's doctor in Pennsylvania from the information you gave me. He will take the stand after you and that should be enough for the jury to see Simon, not as a killer." Kathy watched the faces of Mr. and Mrs. Bradwell light up with hope.

"Oh, before I forget," Kathy interjected. "I went back to talk to one of our witnesses, and I found out something."

"Indeed?" Bailey said intrigued.

"I spoke to Lynn at the Goodwill store, and she may have an alibi for Simon, or at least a partial one."

Bailey leaned forward, "Are you sure?"

"Yes, she said that she would be willing to talk to you only..."

"What?"

"Only she's afraid she might lose her job. I told her that you would help her with that."

Bailey smiled, "If what you say is accurate, I'll do whatever I can."

"Mr. Clark," Mr. Bradwell said. "Whatever help this young lady needs, I'd be more than willing to pay for it."

"Mr. Bradwell, we'll cross that bridge when we get there. For now, I have reserved a room for you and your wife at the Carolina Rose Suites. Go and rest up. It's been a long day," he said as he got up and walked them to the door. As they walked past Kathy, Mr. Bradwell took her by the hand. "Thank you," he said softly as Bailey walked them out of the office. Kathy sat back down in her chair and tried to process everything that had happened. She hoped with all her heart that Bailey was right, but she had first-hand knowledge of what it was like to testify. That D. A. could turn anything you said against you; she hoped that he wouldn't succeed with Mrs. Bradwell or Lynn.

50

Stacey had texted Kathy at four that afternoon to say that she had taken care of dinner. Kathy didn't mind as she had had too much on her mind all day to even think about it. As she opened her apartment door, a familiar smell filled the air.

"Hey Stace, I'm here," Kathy called out making her way to the kitchen table.

"Yeah, in here," Stacey replied. Kathy saw her friend grabbing two soft drinks from the fridge.

"Need any help?"

"Nope, have a seat," she said as they both grabbed a chair. "After my interviews today, I realized what today was, and I thought you could use a food favorite....chicken fried rice."

Kathy smiled, "Thanks, this is perfect." She took the plate Stacey handed her, and it did somehow make her feel better.

"Sorry, I didn't say something this morning."

"Don't worry about it. I took her some flowers and stayed for a minute. It's all I can handle," she said and shrugged it away. "So, speaking of interviews how did they go?"

"Pretty well. I talked to Terrance Williams again and he, like all politicians, was trying to sell all his good points. However, I managed to dig up one or two things that will enlighten our readers," Stacey said triumphantly.

"I am not surprised."

"Oh, and my second interview was very interesting," she hinted as she peered over at her roommate.

"What are you getting at?"

"Not much, only my second interview was with a Benjamin Daniels who just so happens to be the brother of Mark Daniels."

Kathy stopped eating and stared at her best friend, "Wait, Mark Daniels. You mean, Claire Schofield's Mark Daniels."

"One and the same; he got into the race at the last minute. I took a look at his candidate filing and who do you think was his biggest contributor? Yep, none other than his brother. Apparently, the two brothers are fairly close, and I did manage to squeeze the basic family history out of him, but no dirt...yet."

"Well, if you do come across any, please let me know. It could really help expose Claire for who she really is," Kathy said returning to the fried rice in front of her.

"You'll be my first call. So, how was your day?"

"Busy, we might have a break in the case."

"Sounds good."

"Yeah, if the D. A. doesn't twist everything around in court."

"Afraid I can't help you there."

"I know. So, are you ready for the weekend?" Kathy asked as Stacey stopped eating.

"This weekend?"

"Yes, we were going to check out that defense class at the community center tomorrow," Kathy reminded her.

Stacey grimaced, "Kathy, I am so sorry, but I have to write up my interview tomorrow. It's got to be in by lunch."

"Well, I guess you're excused. How about Bri's art show on Sunday?"

"Sunday is good, and who knows there could be an opportunity for a story there." Kathy threw her a look, "And I'll be glad to see Bri's work too."

"You're a trip."

"A reporter's work is never done. Anyway, why don't you ask Michael to go tomorrow morning? If anybody can give you a professional assessment, it's him," she said resuming her dinner.

"You're right."

"Of course, I am."

"And it was his idea in the first place. That settles it," Kathy stated as she put down her fork. "I better see what he says."

"Don't worry," Stacey said as Kathy took out her cell. "All you have to do is ask nicely. There's nothing that officer wouldn't do for you." Kathy smiled and dialed the number.

"Let's see if you're right," she replied as the phone begin to ring. She couldn't wait to hear Michael's reply to this request. Hopefully, he wouldn't try to bail on her too.

Saturday, April 26th

51

It was a beautiful Saturday morning when Kathy finally decided to get up. Kathy lazily got out of bed, put on her locket, and slipped on an old pair of jeans and a T-shirt. Michael said he would pick her up at ten sharp. Kathy noticed the time on her phone read, quarter after nine, so she had plenty of time.

She went to the kitchen, and grabbed a muffin and a cup of coffee. As she looked around for her roommate, she heard a noise coming from the sofa. Kathy walked over to find Stacey asleep on the couch surrounded by notes, a legal pad on the floor, and a pen that had, somehow, rolled under the chin. Kathy stifled a giggle as she took out her phone and took a quick pic. She shook her head and quietly walked back to her muffin on the kitchen table. It wasn't unusual for Stacey to pull all-nighters; Kathy wasn't sure she could handle it. She liked to sleep too much. As she peacefully ate her breakfast, she felt her phone vibrate. She took it out and saw the text from Michael letting her know that he would be there soon. Kathy quietly grabbed her bag from her room and left sleeping beauty undisturbed on the couch. As soon as she made it downstairs, she saw Michael's truck pull up.

"Hey!" he called out from the driver's side, "you need a ride?"

Kathy smiled, "I don't know. You going in my direction," she said walking up to the truck.

"You are my direction," he winked. Kathy laughed and hopped in the truck.

"Good answer," she said and kissed him.

"10-4," he replied and pulled out of the parking lot.

They arrived at the Community Center at quarter to eleven. Kathy was thankful Michael had not followed through with his threat to go in his police uniform. She preferred not to attract that much attention. The Rosemont Community Center was home to many different events. The youth basketball group, summer camp for kids, the site for town auctions, but on Saturdays from eleven a.m. to one p.m., it was the place for Kyle and Paige's self-defense class.

Kathy and Michael walked into the gymnasium and saw several women milling around talking.

"I wonder who's in charge?" Kathy said looking around.

"My guess would be him over there," Michael said pointing to a 5'11" man with brown hair and eyes who did not have an ounce of fat anywhere. Kathy was glad Stacey had decided not to come; she would have been all over this guy. He must have noticed them because he started walking toward them.

"Hi, are you both here for the class," he said with a smile.

"Oh, umm, just me," Kathy replied.

"Well, it's nice to have you. My name is Kyle."

"Kathy," she said shaking his hand.

"I don't believe I saw your name on our sign-up sheet."

"No. I'm just here to check things out. My boyfriend thought it would be a good idea for me."

"I see," Kyle said looking at Michael. "I can tell you probably don't need my class."

Michael gave a sly grin, "I'm an officer with the Rosemont police, so you're right about that." Kathy saw them sizing each other up and quickly broke the silence.

"Would it be alright if we just observe?"

"Absolutely. I lot of first-timers do that. You can grab one of those chairs on the side. If you like what you see, I'd be happy to tell you more about the class."

"Sounds great," Kathy replied as Kyle looked at the gym clock.

"Well, time to get started. You can take a seat over there. I've got a class that's waiting," he said and walked to the front of the gym.

"So, what do you think?" Kathy whispered as they both grabbed a chair to watch.

"We'll see," Michael said noticing everything.

"I know that look officer," Kathy said grinning. "Just don't interrogate him too much. This looks ok to me." Michael didn't respond and all of a sudden she felt sorry for the instructor. She knew that no matter what, he was going to get the third degree when it was over.

52

It had been a slow, quiet morning for David Hamilton. Ever since Kathy had moved out, things had been so different. He had been in his home office all morning going over project lab results and reports. He had told Kathy he would be fine, but that wasn't completely true. There were some days, like yesterday, when the pain in his heart filled his every thought. David stopped what he was doing and leaned his head back to rest his eyes. He was just about to doze off when the phone rang. David looked at the caller ID, but he didn't recognize the number.

"Hello?"

"Is this David Hamilton?" a man's voice said.

"Yes, who is this?"

"Todd Rainor. We spoke earlier about you wanting my help with a case."

David sat up, fully awake, “Yes, yes I did.”

“I wanted to let you know that I have arrived in Rosemont. It’s a nice, friendly place.”

“That was quick,” David said before he had realized he had said that out loud.

“I don’t like to waste time,” Todd replied. “It’s bad for business.”

“Fair enough.”

“I would like for us to meet to get this going, but first I need you to bring two things with you when you come.”

“I’m listening,” David said hoping the requests wouldn’t be too unreasonable.

“I need you to gather all the files and information you have and bring it with you. That way, I can have, hopefully, a decent starting point.”

“Okay, and the other?”

“I’ll need you to bring my fee before I start.”

“You said a thousand dollars, right?”

“Yes,” Todd added.

“Very well, and where do you want to meet?”

“I’m staying at the Rosemont Inn Motel.”

“Why there? The Carolina Rose Suites would be much better.”

“Because the motel will draw less attention and that is my main objective.”

“Of course,” David replied apologetically.

“I’ll be in Room 308. Meet me there tomorrow with what

I asked, and we will proceed."

"Fine; however, I do have one question?"

"Yes?"

"Do you...," David paused trying to find the right words, "have a high success rate?"

"Mr. Hamilton, I understand what you're asking, but I'm afraid you probably won't like my answer. In these cases, cold cases are a roll of the dice. Sometimes they work out and sometimes they don't." David felt a lump grow in his throat. "However, I do successfully close a high percentage of my cases."

"I guess that'll have to do. I will see you tomorrow then," he said and the line went dead. David hung up the phone and stared at the wall. He didn't care about the money; he would give everything he had to find out the truth. David hoped this venture would not be in vain.

53

It was a little after five when Michael drove Kathy back to her apartment. It had been a beautiful day, not a cloud in the sky or maybe, it was the fact that they had spent all day together. They had decided to grab lunch after the self-defense class was over, and then they stopped by the movie theatre.

"So, what do you think?" Kathy asked pulling her hair back in a ponytail.

"I thought it was great. You can't go wrong with a good car chase and that explosion at the end was..."

Kathy laughed, "No. I mean the class."

"Oh, yeah. I think it'll work," Michael said approvingly. "At least you'll be able to get out of some basic situations."

"And it's not that expensive," Kathy added looking at the brochure Kyle had given her on their way out. "His assistant seemed nice."

"Yeah."

"Don't even," Kathy replied, "I know you saw her."

"I plead the fifth," Michael said as Kathy shook her head.

"Anyway, on a better note, are you gonna be free for Bri's art show tomorrow?"

"Sure. Who else is coming?"

"Umm, me, you, and Stacey said she would tag along."

"Stacey, huh?" Michael said with a grin. "Would you mind if I brought my partner along?"

"You wouldn't be trying to start something, would you?"

"Me? Of course not," he said smiling.

"Why not? At any rate, it'll make the day interesting."

"What time?" he asked pulling into one of the parking spaces of the Riverside Complex.

"I'd say noon should be fine," Kathy said putting her bag on her shoulder. "We'll go get some lunch and then, head on over to the gallery."

"Copy that. Hey," he said grabbing her hand. "It was nice seeing you today."

Kathy smiled softly, "Yeah, sometimes it feels like we're just too busy."

"Well, I'm not doing anything right now," he said looking at her intently. Kathy loved the way he looked at her; it made her feel nervous and wonderful all at the same time.

"What are you gettin' at?"

"Come here," he said and gently pulled her closer and

kissed her. As they sat in Michael's truck completely absorbed by one other, Kathy knew she didn't want tonight to end. She could stay right here, with him, forever.

Sunday, April 27th

54

Michael's black Sierra pulled up at noon to pick the girls up for the art show. It was a bit windy, but at least the sun was out. Kathy opened the door and climbed in the backseat with Stacey right behind her. As soon as Stacey noticed Jamie in the passenger seat, she didn't waste any time.

"Well, if it isn't the dream team," she said closing the door. "If I had known, I would've dressed for the occasion." Jamie pulled down the passenger mirror and caught a glimpse, "No problems from what I'm looking at," he said with a smile.

"I knew I liked you," Stacey replied.

"Anyway," Kathy interrupted, "let's go get something to eat."

"10-4. Delany's it is," Michael said as he pulled out of the parking lot.

It seemed like a few minutes later, and they were pulling into the Delany's Pub & Pool Hall parking lot.

"I thought cops were supposed to set an example for all us citizens," Stacey joked as they all got out of Michael's truck.

"Of course, we do," Jamie replied holding the door, "however, Sunday is an exception."

"I should've known," Stacey said with a mocked expression.

"What are we going to do with these two?" Kathy asked as they walked inside and waited to be seated.

"Don't look at me...I think this is hilarious," Michael responded as Sam walked up and showed them to a booth.

"Do you guys know what you want or do you need a minute?" Sam asked fishing out her server book.

"I know what I want," Michael said and Sam began to take their orders.

"So, what's this show we're going to?" Jamie asked.

"It's our friend Brianna," Kathy answered. "This is her first show, and I told her I would bring some people for support."

"Just as long as we don't have to buy something," Jamie said. "Not much of an art person."

"That's okay. You can always pass the time with me," Stacey said as Sam sat their drink orders on the table.

"How is it going, Sam?" Kathy asked.

"Not too bad. It's been a bit slow today. Which is fine by me. I get to stay around the bar," she said as Kathy and Stacey looked at each other and smiled.

"Okay, what did we just miss?" Michael asked.

"Don't worry about it," Sam said. "It's a girl thing."

"Enough said," Jamie conceded as Sam walked back to the bar. It was a few moments later when Sam returned with their order. As they chatted over burgers and fries, Kathy realized this was the first time in a while that they had all been out. It was practically a miracle that she could get her two favorite people together, and Jamie wasn't half bad either.

"Hey," Kathy said looking at her phone. "We need to get going or we're going to be late." Michael waved Sam over and they spilt up the bill. They all climbed back into Michael's truck and headed in the direction of the art gallery.

* * * * * * *

They pulled up to The Rose Art Gallery at five after two. The Rose Art Gallery was a medium-sized building with an all-glass front with 'The Rose' lit up in pinkish neon lights.
As they walked in, they saw Brianna coming toward them in a little black dress, and a small silver belt.

"Hey, you guys," Brianna said with a smile.

"This looks great!" Kathy said giving her friend a hug.

"Thanks. I don't know if I'm nervous, scared, or excited."

"Well, let's see your work," Kathy insisted, and Brianna guided them toward her collection space. There were several paintings, two bronze sculptures, and two portraits. They were all displayed nicely under the gallery track lighting. "These are really good," Kathy said glancing at the collection.

"Thanks. It took me about two years to get these together," Brianna replied beaming with pride. Michael and Jamie remained in the background as the girls chatted over their friend's accomplishments.

"No offense but is there anything else around here?" Jamie finally asked as the girls giggled at their expressions.

"I think there are some bronze panthers over there," Brianna said pointing across the room.

"You go with the guys, Kathy, and I'll stay here and ask our local artist a few questions," Stacey said taking out her recorder.

"Sounds like a plan to me," Kathy said as the three of them headed for the panthers. As they walked over to the bronze sculptures display, Kathy thought she saw a familiar face. She walked to the left to get a better view and couldn't believe what she saw. "You gotta be kidding me," Kathy whispered as the guys came over.

"What is it?" Michael asked as Kathy pointed to a couple standing in front of a huge impressionists painting.

"It's Claire Schofield. What is she doing here?" Kathy muttered.

"Looking at an oversized painting," Jamie commented.

"Who's that guy with her?" Michael asked as his cop instincts started to kick in.

"That's Mark Daniels. The guy she was having an affair

with," Kathy answered. "I can't believe she would show up like this."

"She doesn't seem to mind," Michael observed. Kathy tried not to get too upset, but it just drove her crazy. Here she is in the middle of her husband's murder trial, playing the grieving widow for the jury, and now she's with him in a swanky red dress and heels."

"I can see you're not upset about it," Michael said as Kathy threw him a look.

"It's just not right," Kathy stated. "That painting is probably worth more than what she spent on her husband's funeral."

"It probably is," Brianna said coming up behind them with Stacey in two.

"How much is that painting worth?" Stacey asked.

"That one is a Max Hammond, and his paintings usually go for ten to fifteen thousand dollars," Brianna explained.

"I knew it," Kathy said in disgust as she saw Claire look in her direction. It was all Kathy could do to stay right where she was. Claire gave her a smug smile and wrapped her arm inside Mark's as they moved on to a different painting. Michael noticed that Kathy was starting to really get upset and tried to think of a way to break the staredown.

"Hey, Brianna," Michael said. "Do you have to stay here the whole time, or can you skip out early?"

"I don't have to stay, but I probably need to talk to some of the customers," Brianna said.

"How about we take you to Christine's to celebrate? It's almost four-thirty....how about it?" Michael asked hoping to get Kathy out of there soon.

"Okay," Brianna relented. "Let me go grab my purse, and I'll meet you over there."

"Meet you there," Michael said taking Kathy's hand and guiding her out of the gallery. Kathy couldn't believe what she had just seen. Her husband and Alyssa's father wasnt even cold yet and here she was, living it up with someone else. *You're just cold-blooded*, Kathy thought, *cold through and through.*

55

David Hamilton pulled into the parking lot of the Rosemont Inn Motel. It had taken him a while to gather up the files he had about Colleen's case. It sometimes seemed that that was all he had left of her just some boxes full of what had been. As he knocked on the motel door, he tried not to be nervous even though he had never done anything like this before. On one hand, he was fearful that all this investigator would find would be a big, fat dead-end, but not knowing was even worse.

The door finally opened and a man about 5'10" came into view. David saw that his brown hair looked a bit shaggy, and there was a look in his eyes that made him, for a split-second, question his decision to do this.

"David Hamilton?" he asked closely inspecting his visitor.

"Yes, that's me."

"Come in," he said and opened the door enough for David to squeeze in.

"Have a seat," he pointed to one or two chairs at a small table. David put his briefcase on the table and sat down.

"Thank you for doing this, Mr. Rainor."

"It's Todd, and before we get any further, do you have what I asked?" David pulled out a small manilla envelope.

"A thousand dollars," David said putting it on the table. Todd took the envelope and put it inside his jacket.

"Now, tell me about your wife's case."

"My wife's name is Colleen Hamilton, and she was a therapist. I've gathered all the files I had about her work," he handed Todd a stack of folders he had brought. "Joan Adams was her secretary. I've written her contact information in one of the folders. If anyone would know about my wife's clients, it would be Joan."

"Good," Todd said quickly thumbing through the files.

"This file is all the information I could get on the investigation. A friend in the police department owes me one," David said pulling out a business card from his wallet. "If there's something missing or if you need further information, call this number."

Todd took the card, "Commander James Winters, huh?'

"He said he would help, and he means it."

"So, David, what exactly do you want me to find out?" Todd asked leaning back in his chair.

"I want to know who killed my wife. I want to know

how it was done. I don't understand why the police couldn't find anything."

"Do you mind?" Todd said lighting a cigarette. "David, to be perfectly honest, there's plenty of reasons to choose from as to why this case has gotten cold. Not enough evidence or witnesses or maybe the timing was just wrong. However, this is what I'll do. I will take these files and follow the leads wherever they go and as long as you are willing, I will find who killed your wife. Now, this will probably be a long process. Answers to something like this won't happen overnight."

"Alright," David sighed, deep down he knew Todd was probably right. Just as long as he didn't give up.

"Now, is there anything else I need to know before I get started?" he said pushing the files toward himself.

"Ah, yes," David cleared his throat, "my daughter, Kathy, cannot know about this investigation. I don't want to give her false hope. The first time we went through this was gut-wrenching, and I will not see her go through that again. I will tell her when and only when I have an answer for her."

"You wouldn't happen to have a picture of her?" Todd asked as David opened his wallet and took out a small photo. "Ah, pretty. Don't worry David, I just wanted to know what she looks like so I can avoid her."

"Right, sorry," he said putting the photo back.

"One last thing before I get started. Where do I reach you if I find something?"

"Just call my cell. It's the number I gave you during our

first conversation."

"Good enough," Todd said getting up from the table. "If I need anything else, I will call you; it will be better that way," Todd walked David to the door. "I know it seems like a dead-end now, these kinds of cases always do, but given enough time the truth will come out."

"I hope you're right," he said and they shook hands.

As Todd watched him leave, he couldn't help but notice that his clients were really all the same. Desperate people looking for answers they didn't really want. Todd closed the door and went back to the table to go over the files more closely. He put the patient files to one side and opened the police investigation file. As he scanned the detective's report, a name caught his eye, Detective Winters. "Well, that explains it," he said with a grin. "No wonder this commander is so cooperative." Todd flipped to the witness list, which listed Joan Adams at the top. "Well, Joan, I guess you're the first one on my list too," he said as he wrote down the contact information listed.

56

Dinner at Christine's had gotten everyone in a better mood, even Kathy. It was still windy outside as they filed into Michael's truck and waved goodbye to Brianna. Michael pulled out of the parking lot as Stacey and Jamie struck up another conversation. Kathy watched out the window as the scenery passed her by. It had been a nice change to hang out with her friends; they were all too busy to make it a habit.

As they passed the local motel, Kathy noticed a black car in the parking lot.

"Hey, Stace," she said quickly. "Doesn't that look like my dad's car?" she said as Stacey slid over to look.

"I dunno. There's a lot of black cars around here," she said sliding back into her seat.

"I'd swear that's it," Kathy said looking back at the motel.

"We could run a license check if you want?" Jamie chimed in.

"No, forget he said that," Michael replied with a laugh.

"C'mon Kathy. Why would your dad be at a hotel?" Stacey chided.

"I know! That's what I'm wondering," Kathy replied.

"People meet at motels to have affairs or do shady deals. Your dad doesn't fit either of those descriptions," Stacey added.

"Maybe so, but...."

"Kathy, stop!" Stacey said. "You're making something out of nothing."

Kathy sat back in her seat and shrugged it off. Stacey was probably right; her dad wouldn't do anything shady like that. She was letting that Claire lady get under her skin again she decided as they drove toward Riverside Apartments.

Monday, April 28th

57

It was a cloudy Monday morning as Kathy drove to the office. She pulled up at the stoplight when her phone rang.

"Hello?"

"Hey, Kathy. It's Sally."

"Hey, I'm almost to the parking lot Sally. What is it?"

"Just thought you want to know that Bailey is putting Simon's doctor on the stand today."

"I thought that was for later," Kathy said a bit confused.

"Well, I heard Bailey and Vicky talking on the way out the door, and apparently, Bailey had a change of mind."

"Huh. Umm, Sally, I think I'll drop by the courthouse and see what the doctor has to say," Kathy said turning her car around.

"Okay, see you later," Sally said and hung up. Kathy

pulled into the courthouse parking lot a few minutes later, got out, and locked her car.

As she made her way to the courtroom, she tried to figure out what Bailey was up to. *Had Bailey stumbled onto something?* she wondered. Kathy quietly walked into the courtroom and took a seat on the back row. She saw Bailey, Vicky, and Simon at the defense table. Kathy noticed that there were some new faces present in the gallery. Simon's parents were directly behind him. Mr. Bradwell held his wife's hand as she watched her son, her eyes never left him. Kathy watched as the doctor walked up to take the stand; she held her breath as Bailey stood up.

"Would you please state your name for the record?"

"Dr. Daniel Carrey."

"Now, Dr. Carrey what is your specialty as a doctor?"

"I am a neurologist with the Ashbury Clinic in Pennsylvania.'"

"How long have you treated the defendant, Simon Bradwell?"

"Mr. Bradwell started seeing me about a year ago." Kathy slid over in her seat to get a better look. Dr. Carrey was a middle-aged man with salt-and-pepper hair. He wore rimless glasses and spoke in an authoritative tone. He would need that when the D.A. got ahold of him.

"And what was your initial diagnosis?"

"Mr. Bradwell came to me, initially, with severe headaches and some confusion. I decided to run several tests, and I concluded that Simon Bradwell had a brain tumor." Kathy heard some muffled sounds coming from Simon's mother in the gallery. She couldn't imagine what his parents were going through right now.

"Dr. Carrey, would that explain Simon's unusual behavior?"

"Yes. Simon's aversion to being around people, forming connections with his possessions, and easily feeling threatened are all signs of his medical condition."

Kathy sat there and listened to every word the doctor said. With that kind of testimony, no jury in their right mind could convict Simon. Kathy decided that she had heard enough. She quietly slipped out of the courtroom and decided to get some fresh air.

58

Kathy decided to leave the courthouse drama behind her and get a new perspective on things. As she sat down on one of the wooden benches in the park, she took a deep breath and instantly felt better. There were joggers and bikers on the park trails. A family with two small children were feeding the ducks near the lake. Kathy looked around as her mind began to wonder. She thought back to the Chase Wanger case and how everything pointed to Chase, but Kathy knew that he didn't do it, just like Simon. *Everything points to him, but he didn't kill Charlie. So, if both of these guys are innocent then who was or is the real killer?* Kathy thought. She remembered her last phone call with Charlie and how he had said that someone was after him. *Is that person the real killer? How do I find someone that nobody has seen?* Kathy looked in her bag for her phone and found the mystery note.

No good deed goes unpunished. "The real killer sent this note to me," she whispered. "For some reason, the killer wanted me to know, but why?" Kathy sat looking at the note, trying to solve the puzzle. *This note is all I have, so I'll start there,* she thought to herself. *I'll get every bit of information I can from it, and then maybe, I'll have something that will lead me to him.* She carefully put the note back in her bag filled with a new purpose.

59

David Hamilton was sitting on the living room couch, watching the news at noon. He had resisted the urge, several times, to call Todd and ask about his progress; waiting was something he was not good at, especially when there was so much at stake. He had argued with himself about whether or not he had made the right decision of hiring an investigator. How he wished he had someone to talk to about this. He looked on the mantle and saw Colleen's eyes shining back at him. He slowly got up, retrieved the picture from the mantle, and sat back down. "Hey, sweetheart," he said holding the picture in his hand. "I wish you were here. I've hired an investigator to find out what happened to you. I hope I've hired the right one; he seemed like he knew what he was doing." David looked at his wife's face and knew what she would've said. "I know you don't like me keeping things from Kathy. You didn't do things like that, but Colleen, it's for the best. I'll tell her everything once I have an answer; I promise, sweetheart. I only hope this investigator doesn't play me for a fool. Am I just grasping at straws? Am I doing the right thing?" He stared at the picture in from of him, waiting for a sign of approval, anything to let him know this was the right thing to do. He sighed and gently put her picture back on the mantle.

As he grabbed the remote to turn off the TV, he noticed that the news had ended, and a movie was coming on. For some reason, he stood there as the opening credits came on the screen. David dropped the remote and choked up when the movie title flashed across the screen, "Let Me Call You Sweetheart." He couldn't believe it, what were the odds. He let the movie play as he looked back at his wife's picture and whispered, "Thank you."

60

Kathy walked back into her office around one o'clock. She closed the door and went directly to her caseboard. She drew a comparison chart and wrote Sandy Malone on one side and Charlie on the other. Then, she pulled out her notes from both cases and started writing down the similarities. "Okay," she began, "both cases had evidence pointing to somebody else like Chase Wagner and now, Simon. Both cases were short on eyewitnesses to the actual crime, and the victims in both cases appear to be connected." Kathy wrote down each similarity on her caseboard and stepped back to think. "So, what kind of person would do this? Was it one person, maybe or maybe not? One thing is certain they knew how to cover their tracks, so..." Kathy pondered. "They've probably done this before." She went to her bag and pulled out the mystery note. She wasn't sure where to begin, but she knew someone who might as she pulled out her cell phone.

"This is Stacey."

"Yes, I'm looking for Rosemont's finest journalist to help me with a specific problem," Kathy said grinning.

'Wow, not bad. You could've added brilliant or fashionable, but not bad. So, what do you need?"

Kathy laughed, "Do you have any connections with anyone with handwriting analysis?"

"Huh, well that sounds interesting."

"C'mon, Stace."

"I might know of someone who possibly does that kind of thing."

"Any chance you have contact information?"

"Yeah, just not on me. It's back at the apartment in my Rolodex. I'll text it to you as soon as I get back."

"Stace, you're the best."

"True."

"I'll owe you one."

"Just give me the details when you can."

Kathy smiled, "Deal," she said and hung up. She grabbed one of the plastic bags from her desk drawer, placed the note inside, and pinned it to the caseboard. Kathy went back to her desk and looked through her Chase Wagner notes. When she came across the article about 'The Night Lounge', she stopped and re-read the article. Kathy looked at the caseboard, then back at the article in her hand. She grabbed a pen and circled the words 'The Night Lounge' and 'i guardiani.' "I need to find out who or what this is," she said as she flipped open her laptop and typed in i guardiani in the search box. She clicked on the news tab and scrolled through the results. Kathy couldn't believe her eyes; from everything she was reading, i guardiani was the name of a crime organization. According to the news articles, they were suspected of having ties to gambling, blackmail, bribery, and murder. "Well, that's just great," Kathy said as she started to print out the articles.

As the printer began to hum away, she grabbed a piece of paper and drew an organizational chart. "I need to figure out who these people are, and why there seems to be a connection to these two cases." Kathy went to the printer, stapled each article together, and put them in a folder she titled 'i guardiani'. She went back to her laptop when her stomach started to growl. Between the courtroom this morning and following her leads, she had completely forgotten about food. She looked at her cell which read three o'clock. "No wonder I'm hungry," Kathy said feeling famished. "I wonder if Stacey is back at the apartment yet," she wondered sending her a quick text. Kathy began to clean up her desk when her phone buzzed. She swiped the lock screen and saw the text from Stacey.

Be there n 10 mins.

You hungry?

Sure.

I'll pick up subs on my way.

C you soon.

Kathy started to put her cell away when it occurred to her that she hadn't heard from her dad lately. It wasn't like him to not at least say hello. Kathy dialed the number and waited on the line.

"Hello, Hamilton residence."

"Hey, Dad."

"Oh, hello to you," Kathy thought he sounded a bit off.

"I just realized it's been a while since I've talked to you and just wanted to see what's going on."

"I'm alright. The house is a little too quiet sometimes, but I'm okay."

"Been anywhere lately?" Kathy asked trying to sound casual.

"I visited your mom recently."

"Yeah, I know. I did too," Kathy confessed.

"Oh, I see what this is. You're checking up on me."

"Well..."

"Kathleen, I appreciate the concern, but I'm fine. I do wish you would come over for dinner again."

"Okay, it's a deal. Talk to you later."

"Bye," he said and hung up.

Kathy put her phone away and scolded herself. How could she possibly think that her dad was hiding something? *He wouldn't do that,* she told herself as she finished putting her desk in order. Kathy said goodbye to Sally on her way out. She had an appointment with Rosemont's finest journalist and a ham and cheese sub.

Tuesday, April 29th

61

Kathy pulled into the parking lot later than usual. After a long night of discussing her theory with Stacey, she had decided to sleep in the next morning. She walked into the law office and saw Sally at the desk putting away some files.

"Morning, Sally," Kathy said leaning on the reception desk.

"A bit late this morning."

"I pulled a late night. Is Bailey already in court?" Kathy asked changing the subject.

"Yeah, closing arguments are today."

"Did Bailey say how the case is going?"

"Not really, although he did stay pretty late last night working on his closing arguments."

"Well, if they're anything like his opening statement, it

should turn out right," Kathy said wanting to believe her own words.

"Oh, before you leave today don't forget to turn in your log sheet."

"Right, will do," Kathy replied as she left Sally at her desk, and she headed off to hers.

Kathy opened the door and sat her bag on the desk. She pulled out her notepad and started up the laptop. "Okay," she began, "let's see if I can't make some more progress today." She pulled up her email and typed in the email address Stacey gave her for Ian Richardson.

After several revisions, Kathy read the message one more time, and finally satisfied, pressed the send button. "Now, that's done let's see those articles again." Kathy had gone through them once last night with a highlighter, marking anything that might be important. As she looked over her markings, questions started to swirl around in her head. She turned to a blank page in her notepad and grabbed a pen. One of the articles she went through last night, had two names mentioned so Kathy had made sure that she circled them. One was Brett Avery, a lawyer for the organization and the other was Luca Rizzo. Kathy had googled the lawyer and discovered that he had graduated from Harvard Law School and had been working for the organization for about six years. She had printed out what information she could find, along with a picture, and added it to her file. Luca Rizzo was a different story, information on this guy was slim to non-existent. She took out her organizational chart of i guardiani and wrote the two names to the side. "Now, how do they fit in? And who is the head of this organization?" She sighed and glanced over at her caseboard. *Why Sandra and Charlie?* she wondered. Sandra must have been a witness to something she shouldn't have seen, and Charlie died because he saw what happened to Sandra. Kathy leaned against her desk, looking at the plethora of information in front of her. "How do I find out what Sandra saw?" For a spilt- second, she thought about asking Bailey, but shot that down quick. It would be better to have something concrete before going to Bailey. Kathy looked at the crime scene photos from Charlie's murder and suddenly, a thought struck her. "Wait a minute, Charlie said someone was following him the last time he called me. Where did he call from?" she asked quickly flipping through her notes. "Freddie's Quickstop." Kathy thought for a moment and then shoved her things in her bag. "There's something at the Quickstop that I missed, and this time, I'm not leaving until I figure out what it is," she said as she hurried out the door.

62

After an hour of heated persuasion, Bailey had finally arranged for Mr. & Mrs. Bradwell to see their son. He guided them back to the holding cell, where Simon was waiting to be transported back to the jail. It had been a very emotional day in court. Mrs. Bradwell had barely made it through her testimony, luckily the D.A. had decided not to cross.

As they approached the holding cell, they saw Simon back in the orange jumpsuit seated at the table, wearing a pair of handcuffs. The guard stood outside as Bailey led them in.

"Simon," Bailey said. "Your parents are here to see you." Simon didn't move, he just kept his head down. Mr. & Mrs. Bradwell sat down across from her son. For years she had dreamed and hoped to find him, but never did she imagine in a jail cell.

"Simon," she whispered. "Please say something." Simon seemed determined to stare down at the table. "Simon, do you remember the story I used to read to you when you were little?" Simon just sat there. "It was about a Mama Bear and her Baby Bear. Do you remember what the mama bear would say when the baby bear asked her a question?" Simon started to squirm in his seat. "She said, 'I love you forever...'"

"To the moon and back," Simon said softly as he finally lifted up his head. Mrs. Bradwell saw the tears welling up in his eyes and gently placed her hands over his.

"Exactly. To the moon and back," she said smiling as tears started to run down her cheeks.

"Oh, Mom, I'm so sorry," Simon said as he broke down in tears.

"It's ok," she said gripping his hands tightly. "It's okay."

"I was scared," Simon sobbed. "I couldn't face it. I just wanted to escape. I know you're both upset with me."

"Simon," Mr. Bradwell said as he knelt beside his son. "My boy, we are not upset. We only want you to be safe."

"You're not mad?" Simon asked wiping away his tears.

"We love you, and as soon as we can, we are going to take you home and take care of you," Mr. Bradwell said trying to keep his composure.

"Am I really going home?" Simon asked hopefully as they all turned and looked at Bailey. Bailey hated questions like this because there was no guarantee that it would turn out the way they wanted.

"I try not to give my clients false hope, but I will say this. If the jury listened to our evidence and believes that we have told them the truth, then there is no reason why they would find you guilty."

"Time's up," the guard said as two more officers walked up to take Simon back to the jail. As they said their goodbyes, Bailey put on a brave face. He didn't give his clients false hope, but he just didn't have the heart to spoil their moment. He had given the jury every opportunity to doubt the state's case against his client. He hoped the jury would do the right thing, but he knew from experience that juries can be unpredictable.

63

Kathy pulled into Freddie's Quickstop a little after four and walked inside. She looked around, saw one man in the back, and one attendant behind the counter. It wasn't Sophie, Kathy noticed. It looked like the guy that was here last time. Kathy flipped through her notepad and found the name, Tyler, written down. She flipped to a new page and walked up to the counter.

"Hi. My name is Kathy. I was here before talking with Sophie," Kathy said hoping he would remember.

"Right," he said nodding his head. "You were asking questions about something."

"That's right, but I wanted to ask you if you noticed anything strange on Thursday the 17th?" Tyler thought about it for a moment.

"I'm not sure. I was dealing with this piece of junk, again," he said pointing at the receipt printer. "It wouldn't print nothing, but come to think of it, one of the regulars, he usually comes every Tuesday, showed up on Thursday, pretty late."

"Really. I wasn't aware that gas stations have regulars."

"Sure, we do. They keep coming back because of our sparkling personalities, and speaking of," Tyler said pointing outside. "There he is now." Kathy turned around as a black Lexus pulled up to one of the pumps. A man in his mid-thirties, sandy hair, and glasses, got out.

"Thanks for your help," Kathy said as she walked out of the Quickstop and hopefully, to her next lead. The man was filling up his car when Kathy walked over. "Excuse me," she said as he looked in her direction. "My name is Kathy Hamilton. I'm an investigator for Bailey Clark. I was wondering if I could ask you a few questions." The man had a puzzled look on his face but just shrugged his shoulders.

"Why not."

"Thank you. The attendant inside says that you usually come on Tuesdays."

"Huh. I never thought about it, but I guess I do."

"He also said that last week you came on a Thursday instead." The man leaned against his car and thought for a minute.

"Oh, I remember. I did come on a Thursday that week. My meetings ran over, and everything went down from there."

"When you came that Thursday, do you remember seeing

this man here?" Kathy asked and held up a picture of Charlie.

He looked at the picture, "He does look familiar."

"So, you've seen him?" Kathy asked trying to stay calm.

"He looks like the homeless guy I saw at the payphone that day. He looked upset; he kept looking around and then, he ran out of the phonebooth."

"Did you see which direction he went?"

"No," he said shaking his head. "I was watching the other one." Kathy couldn't believe her ears.

"What other one?"

"There was a second guy that came after the homeless man."

"You wouldn't happen to remember what he looked like?"

"He was wearing a dark coat, tall, and..."

"What?"

"I don't know, just something about him didn't feel right."

"Did you notice anything else?" she asked making some notes in her notepad.

"Not really. He didn't go near the payphone. He just slowly followed the homeless man."

"Really?"

"I mean I would've done something, but I didn't know what. It had been such a long day. I just wanted to finally get home."

"Do you mind if I get your name and number?"

"Sure. Name is Brad Simpson, and my cell is 910-336-

2784." Kathy jotted down the contact information and put her notepad away.

"Mr. Simpson, thank you so much. You have been a huge help."

"Yeah, whatever," Brad said as he left and went inside the Quickstop. Kathy couldn't believe what she had just heard. This guy actually saw Charlie just before he died and caught a glimpse at the real killer. Kathy walked back to her car in a slight daze when she heard a noise. She snapped out of it and picked up her cell.

"Hello?"

"Kathy, it's Bailey."

"Oh, hey Bailey."

"I just wanted to let you know that the jury has begun deliberations."

"Oh, is that good or bad?" Kathy asked not sure if she really wanted an answer.

"I'll tell you what I told Simon's parents. I've given the jury plenty of reasons to find Simon innocent if they take it."

"Oh, how did they take it?"

"Pretty well. I finally got them in to see Simon."

"I'm sure they appreciated that."

"Well, we will find out shortly."

"Guess so."

"See you tomorrow," he said and hung up. Kathy got inside her car and decided to call Stacey about food arrangements. They were in for another long night.

64

Bailey had thought about going home but went back to the office instead. He dropped his briefcase on the floor and flopped in his chair. He enjoyed the silence of his office after the courtroom drama of the day. Bailey had sent Vicky home after court to get some rest; he, however, could not rest. There was still too much on his mind. The D.A.'s closing statement was still playing in his mind. As much as he hated to admit it, Phillips knew what he was doing. He had given the jury quite a picture of Simon as a killer. Bailey had watched the jury during the D.A.'s monologue, jurors numbers three and six worried him. They never took their eyes off Simon, and he still wasn't sure if that was good or bad. He propped his head in his hands and tried to clear his head. It was done; he had given Simon his best shot; he hoped it would be enough. Watching Simon's parents tell their son that he was coming home had made Bailey choke up. The jury had to find him innocent, they simply had to. He was not going to let that family get torn apart again.

Wednesday, April 30th

65

Kathy reluctantly woke up the next morning and cut off her alarm. She had been up late again last night with Stacey working on her theory. After agreeing that the two cases were connected, they had tried to think of ways to find out more about the i guardiani crime organization, but the options were slim. Kathy had suggested trying to call in a favor with Michael and Stacey said she could see if her fellow reporters knew anything. They went over all the evidence that Kathy had collected so far and decided to see what the handwriting analysis report said first. She glanced at her phone and noticed that Mr. Richardson had replied to her email. She got up, slipped on a pair of jeans, dark green shirt, and clasped on her locket. She picked up her cell and headed for the kitchen.

She grabbed a cup of coffee and a blueberry muffin

and took a seat at the table. She hadn't expected Mr. Richardson to respond so quickly. She opened her email on her cell and navigated to the email in question.

Ms. Hamilton,
I thank you for your interest in my services. I am available to look at the document in question. My fee for rendering said services is $600. This will include a complete analysis of the document and a report of my findings. Please send the document via certified mail to Dr. Ian Richardson, P.O. Box 30372 Fairfax, VA 22030. Payment options can be found at www.richarsondocumentexpert.com. I will let you know when I have received the document. If you have any questions please respond, to this email.

Kathy sighed and took a sip of her coffee. "$600, huh," she said, thinking to herself. She would have to move some things around to come up with that much money. Then, she suddenly had a thought, *Maybe, Dad could loan me some of the money.* She looked at the clock on her phone which read nine o'clock. She needed to get to the office, just in case Bailey called. She finished her muffin and grabbed her bag from her room. The jury was still out, and Kathy hoped that Bailey got through to them. She hated to think what would happen to Simon if he didn't.

66

It was a cloudy and windy morning when Kathy walked into the office. The weatherman on the radio said there was a chance of rain; Kathy hoped he was wrong.

"Hey, Sally," Kathy said as Sally looked up.

"Hey."

"Did they already leave?" Kathy asked pulling up a chair next to the reception desk.

"Yep, Bailey and Vicky left at eight-thirty to meet Simon's parents at the courthouse."

"Bailey didn't happen to mention what he thought the jury would do?"

"All he said was that he gave the jury plenty of reasons to doubt the state's case, but..."

"But what?" Kathy asked nervously.

"He did say that he didn't like the behavior of juror numbers three and six."

"Why, what does that mean?"

"Something about how they kept staring at Simon."

"I didn't need to know that," Kathy groaned.

"Well, you asked."

Kathy held up her hand, "I know, I know. Did they say that they would let us know the verdict?"

"Uh-huh. As soon as it comes in, Vicky said she would call the office."

"Well, then I guess I'm not going anywhere," she said getting comfortable in her chair.

"And here I thought you enjoyed my company," Sally said with a mocked look of hurtfulness.

"To change the subject, do you mind if I run something by you?"

"Sure, hit me," Sally said with genuine interest.

"Do you remember our previous case, the Chase Wagner case?"

"Uh-huh, what about it?"

"Do you think it seems kind of similar to this one?" Kathy asked giving Sally a sideways glance.

"Oh, well, I don't know. I guess I had never really thought about it. Why, do you think so?"

"There are similarities in these two cases that just don't sit right with me."

"Have you told Bailey?"

"I don't really have enough concrete evidence for that right now," Kathy confessed. "Hey, does Bailey keep experts on the payroll?"

"Yeah, he has a few," Sally said grabbing the Rolodex on her desk. "Let's see there's a psychologist, forensic guy, a doctor, and a government consultant, whatever that means."

"Huh," Kathy said with a frown.

"What are you fishing for?" Sally asked with a grin.

"It doesn't matter now."

"Aww, c'mon. You can tell me."

"I was just looking for options on how to prove my theory, that's all."

"Oh, I see. By the way, do you have your log sheet for this case?"

"Yeah, hang on," Kathy said as she dug around in her bag and handed Sally the completed log. Sally smiled and looked at the log.

"You know you keep these hours up, and you'll be working just as much as Bailey does," she said filing the log sheet away.

"So, I take it that Bailey doesn't have much of a personal life," Kathy asked grateful to change the subject.

"I've never heard him talk of one. Not a family or special someone, just work, and clients."

"I wonder why?" Kathy mused aloud. "I mean Bailey's good-looking, makes good money, and he's a nice guy. Why wouldn't he have someone?"

"I agree, and I would generally be the first to find out why; however, I don't like to bit the hand that feeds me."

"So, you do have limits," Kathy said smiling.

"Just a few. I mean I like good gossip with the best of them, but I also want to keep my job."

"Very sensible," Kathy said looking at the office clock. "Good grief, it's getting close to eleven."

"And no news yet," Sally said with a worried look.

"I hope that's not a bad sign," Kathy said as they both looked at each other thinking the worst.

67

Bailey had tried to sit on one of the benches outside of the courtroom, waiting patiently, but he couldn't take it anymore. He slowly paced back and forth while Vicky and Mr. Bradwell sat with Simon's mother. Bailey could almost hear the minutes tick by, at ten sharp, Bailey had asked Vicky to check on the jury, but when she returned, she just shook her head no. She sat back down on the bench, and they continued to wait.

"How much longer?" Mrs. Bradwell moaned. Simon's parents looked at Bailey waiting for an explanation.

"It's hard to say, hopefully not much longer," he said with a forced smile. "If we don't hear anything in the next few minutes, we'll go get something to eat, and Vicky will notify the court."

"Oh, I couldn't eat anything," Mrs. Bradwell sobbed.

"Not until I know what's going to happen to my son."

"Don't worry," her husband said putting his arm around her shoulders. "It'll turn out alright. We have the best lawyer right here."

Bailey smiled, but inside he was starting to worry himself. With all the evidence he gave this jury, it shouldn't take this long. Bailey eyed the courtroom and secretly wondered what he could've done differently.

68

Kathy had returned to the office a little after two with their lunch orders, just as a small rain shower started to fall.

"Made it," Kathy said hurrying inside so the food wouldn't get wet.

"Just in time," Sally replied putting away some files. "I just finished catching up on the office bills." Kathy came around the reception desk and took a seat beside Sally.

"Here ya go. Double cheeseburger and fries for you," she said giving Sally her order. "And a McChicken and fries for me."

"Smells good. I'm starved," Sally replied quickly opening the bag.

"Any phone calls?" Kathy asked as she opened her bag.

Sally sighed, "No. I thought I was going to burn a hole in that phone, so I decided to get something done instead."

"This isn't looking good for us, is it?" Kathy said eating a fry.

"I don't...," Sally stopped mid-sentence as the office phone began to ring. Kathy and Sally both froze as Sally slowly picked up the receiver.

"Bailey Clark's office."

"Sally, it's Vicky."

"Hey Vicky, what happened?" Sally asked preparing for the worst.

"Sally, we did it!"

"What?"

"The jury came back with a not-guilty verdict."

"Holy crap!" Sally exclaimed as Kathy jumped out of her chair.

"Tell Kathy, we'll be at the office as soon as we finish up here."

"Okay, okay. I will," Sally replied and hung up the phone.

"Sally, tell me right now, what happened?" Kathy said bursting with anticipation.

"They did it, they got Simon off!" Sally shouted as they both hugged each other.

"Thank God," Kathy said relieved.

"Vicky said they're all coming back to the office, so..."

"So what?"

"Let's finish eating and come up with a surprise."

"I like it," Kathy said smiling as they began to hatch a plan.

* * * * * * * *

It was a little after three when Bailey and company made it back to the office. He walked through the door to find the lights off and nobody around.

"Hey, Vicky, I thought you said they would be waiting for us?" Bailey asked as they all came in and shut the door.

"That's what Sally said. Let me find the light and..." before Vicky could finish the office lights came on and Kathy and Sally jumped up from behind the desk.

"Surprise!" they shouted as the unexpected guests jumped back a little. Now that Bailey and the rest could see, they looked and saw a silver congratulations banner hanging from the ceiling, several glasses sitting on the reception desk, and a bottle of wine.

"What is going on here?" Bailey asked sitting his briefcase down.

"We thought you all deserved a treat after a long, hard fight," Kathy said as Sally grabbed the bottle.

"You scared me half to death," Vicky replied taking the glass Sally handed her.

"I'm just glad it's over," Mrs. Bradwell said holding tight to her son's hand.

"Yes, and now we finally get to go home as a family," Mr. Bradwell replied taking the glass Sally offered him. "I would like to make a toast. Here's to Bailey Clark and Associates," he said raising his glass, "the best law office around."

"Here, here," Kathy and Sally shouted.

"Also, I would like to add our sincere thanks to Ms. Kathy Hamilton for finding our son. There are no words, thank you," he said as his eyes started to moisten.

"Oh, you're welcome. I'm just glad it turned out right," Kathy said smiling.

"What's next for the three of you?" Bailey asked taking a sip of the wine.

"We are going home to get Simon the treatment he needs. Our flight leaves soon, so we have to be going."

"We understand completely," Bailey said shaking his hand. "Good luck to all of you.""

Mr. and Mrs. Bradwell smiled as they left with their son, now a whole family. As they left, Vicky whispered something to Bailey.

"Yes, I think you're right," he said as she went into her office and returned with a small package.

"What's going on?" Kathy asked.

"Since we're celebrating, I think now is the perfect time for this," he said as Vicky handed the small package to Kathy.

"It was supposed to be ready when we went to Christine's for the Chase Wagner case, but it wasn't quite ready," Vicky said smiling. Kathy looked at the small package wrapped in plain, brown paper. She slowly began to tear away the wrapping, and then she saw what was inside.

"That is for a job well done," Bailey added with a smile. Kathy started to tear up, she held in her hands a mahogany, gold-plated nameplate that read: Kathy Hamilton, Investigator.

"It's beautiful. Thank you."

"I think it will fit nicely on your desk," Bailey said taking another sip of his wine. "Well, I think we all deserve congratulations. We did our jobs and the law prevailed. Now, I am going home to get some long overdue sleep," he said as he sat down his glass and waved goodbye.

"We'll clean up here," Vicky said as Bailey headed for home. "I'm glad this one's done," she sighed as she and Sally began to take down the banner. Kathy looked at the nameplate she was holding and knew they were wrong. *It's not over*, she thought to herself, *there are still too many loose ends, and I'm going to find out where they lead,* she promised herself as she began to help the others cleanup for the day.

Epilogue

Winchester slung his duffel bag over his shoulder and walked out of his motel room. He had gotten the call he'd been waiting for. He returned his key at the front desk and walked out. As he stepped outside into the fresh air, he took one last look at this small town. It was a nice day, not a cloud in the sky, and full of possibilities. This town held some memories for him, ones he would never forget. He took a small photo out of his pocket and thought about the girl with the pretty black hair. *It's a shame I didn't have more time*, he thought putting the photo back as he walked to his black SUV. *Don't worry pretty girl...I mean Kathy Hamilton. I'll be back; I'm not done with you, not by a long shot,* he thought as an evil smile crept onto his face. "You'll find out soon enough that no good deed goes unpunished," he said as he pulled out of the parking lot and drove away.

ACKNOWLEDGEMENTS

Here I am writing the last pages of book three in the Kathy Hamilton series, and I am amazed how far I have come from a little girl with a dream to an author publishing her third novel. I am so excited and grateful. There are several people I need to thank because all of this wouldn't have been possible without them.

First of all, I want to thank God for giving me the talent, imagination, and ability to write this series. For opening doors and opportunities for me that I could never imagine. I am truly blessed and thankful for all He has done.

To my mom, who is always there when I need her. She is the best support I could ever ask for. Thank you for your encouragement, proofing my rough drafts for the hundredth time, and for being my on-call sounding board. I truly appreciate everything you have done. Thank you for such wonderful support.

I would also like to thank my publisher, Bookbaby, who has made it possible for me to bring my ideas to print. Their editing services and customer support have truly been wonderful. Thank you for helping me make my writing dreams come true.

To my First Baptist Reading Circle, I would like to say thank you for your support, suggestions, and advice. It's so nice to have people you can go to and receive such invaluable advice. I truly appreciate the time and energy you have given to me.

Lastly, I would like to thank you, the reader, for purchasing my book. I have tried to create a series that you can truly enjoy and get lost in. I hope I have succeeded in giving you that kind of reading experience. I hope you will come back for the next Kathy Hamilton installment.

To find out more about me or my novels, please visit my website: www.authormaggiecasteen.com. You can also find me on Facebook, Instagram, and Goodreads.

Thank you.

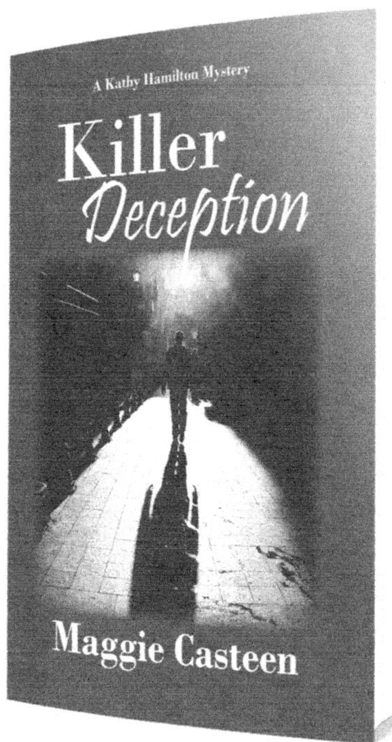
A Kathy Hamilton Mystery
Killer
Deception
Maggie Casteen

AVAILABLE NOW

Look out for the next chapter

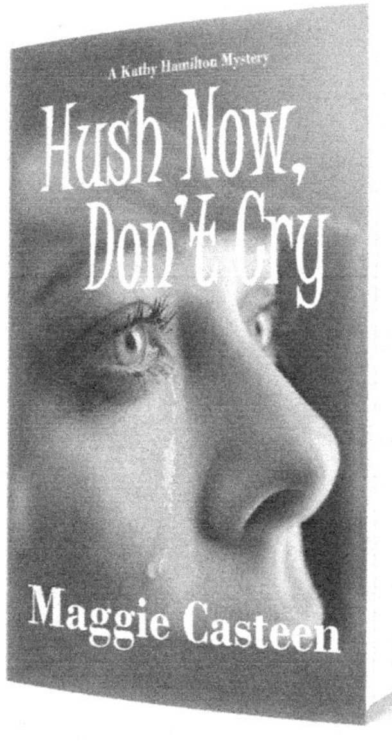

A Kathy Hamilton Mystery
Hush Now, Don't Cry
Maggie Casteen

In the next installment of the Kathy Hamilton Mystery series a lot of changes are coming for Kathy. After a successful trip in the UK with the Brooks case, Kathy is back home in Rosemont and looking for a chance to work as an investigator. A local defense attorney, Bailey Clark, decides to give her a chance, but her first case could be her last. The client is accused of killing a young woman outside of Delany's Bar, but the only thing is he can't remember what happened. Did he do it or is something more sinister at work underneath? Kathy will follow the clues to discover the truth...if it's not too late.

Sign Up for Maggie's Newsletter

Keep up to date with book releases, awesome book leads and feature articles by signing up for her email list at.....

www.authormaggiecasteen.com

You will also receive my FREE prequel story

A DEADLY DECEPTION

Find me on Facebook.
facebook.com/maggiecasteen/05

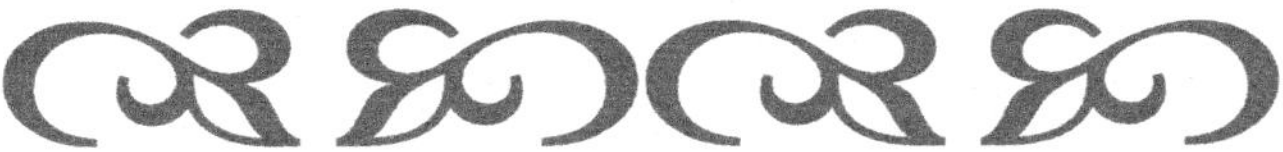